THE ASCENDANTS

BOOK TWO - WARRIORS OF THE WAY

ORLANDO SANCHEZ

Other titles by Orlando Sanchez

The Spiritual Warriors

Blur-A John Kane Novel

The Deepest Cut-A Blur Short

The Last Dance A Sepia Blue Short

THE ASCENDANTS

Copyright © 2015 by Orlando Sanchez.

OM Publishing NY NY

For information contact: www.nascentnovel.com

Book and Cover design by Derek Murphy
http://www.creativindiecovers.com

ISBN: 9781507684047

D1713597

First Edition: January 2015

10 9 8 7 6 5 4 3 2 1

The Warrior's Creed

I will train my heart and body for an unmovable spirit.

I will pursue the true meaning of the warrior's way, so that in time my senses may be alert.

With true vigor I will cultivate a spirit of selflessness.

I will observe the rules of courtesy, respect my elders and refrain from violence.

I will follow my spiritual principles, never forgetting the true virtue of humility.

I will look upwards to wisdom and strength, forsaking other desires.

All my life, I will seek to fulfill the true meaning of the warrior's way.

ONE

THE DOJO SMELLED OF SWEAT and old wood. The morning sun glistened on the hardwood floor creating pools of brilliance. In the center of the floor stood a figure. His white hair was cut short. His gnarled hands clasped gently in meditation rested on the knot of his *obi* the belt that designated him as the sensei of the school. His uniform hid his frame, muscled from years of extreme training. His breaths were so measured it seemed he wasn't breathing.

Every morning he stood there, waiting for the sun to rise. As the sunlight touched his feet, he exploded in movement. His body moved with grace and power. Each strike was precise and deadly. He did this *kata* a prearranged set of movements every day since he learned it three hundred years ago. It was in his body now. He no longer needed to think about the movements. They flowed of their own volition. A dance of life and death. He finished his last move facing away from the entrance as another figure entered the dojo.

He was taller than the sensei. His long black hair was tied into a ponytail. Two swords were strapped to his back, the hilts of which protruded past his shoulders, giving the impression of horns. He stepped onto the dojo floor, his leather boots creaking softly. His every step spoke menace.

"I see you haven't lost your ability, sensei," said the figure.

The sensei spoke without turning. With his senses expanded he knew it was Rael.

"That title is no longer applicable to you. How did you escape?"

"Funny thing, that. It seems ascendants are dying, *sensei*," said Rael.

The sensei remained motionless.

"Dying or being killed?"

"Does it matter? The end result is the same and here I am," said Rael with a mock bow.

"You will go back, Harbinger," said the sensei in a quiet voice.

"Are you going to send me? Are you strong enough?" said Rael as he unsheathed his swords. Dark blue energy enveloped the blades, crackling with power. The smell of burning metal filled the dojo as he extended his arms to the side.

"Our strength does not diminish with age. You most of all should know that."

The sensei turned to face Rael. He held a folded metal fan in each hand.

"Where is he, sensei? The one who carries the weapon?"

"He is not here." The sensei flicked his wrists, opening the fans.

"But you know where he is," said Rael. "All of you are connected on some level. You know where he is."

He brought his swords to his sides and the energy arced between them, setting off small lightning strikes across the dojo floor. Rael approached the sensei, gliding forward with unnatural speed, his fans giving off silver light as he advanced. Rael slashed with both swords, crossing them. Flicking a fan closed as he ducked, the sensei stopped the attack, immobilizing Rael's forearms. Energy bathed them as Rael twisted back, out of the hold.

"Stop this, Rael," said the sensei as he stepped back. "You cannot help your master. It would be the end of everything." Rael took a defensive stance, his swords burning the air around them.

"*Help* him? You say that like I have a choice. He *owns* me, sensei. Just tell me where Dante is. I know you know."

"I cannot."

"Before you die today, you will."

Rael stepped back and sheathed his swords as three figures entered the dojo. Standing seven feet tall, their muscular bodies rippled with dark energy as they stepped onto the dojo floor. Two of them held metal spheres attached to a chain, the third held a little girl.

"Grandpa, are these big men your friends?" said the little girl.

"Her parents?" asked the sensei.

Rael walked over and took the little girl's hand and squatted down to look in her eyes. A chain and bell materialized in the giant's hand as she let go.

"They didn't make it," said Rael. "Did you know her father was an ascendant?"

The sensei narrowed his eyes.

"Gyrevex," said the sensei. "You dared to summon them?"

"I wonder if she is an ascendant?" said Rael as he stroked her hair. Rael walked over to the Gyrevex nearest him, tapping him on the chest as he spoke.

"Turns out I didn't need three of these," said Rael. "One of them is like an army, unfeeling, uncaring. Practically impossible to stop. He gave me three—talk about overkill."

"She is not part of this. Let her go," said the sensei.

"If she was an ascendant it would be too early to tell. What's your name, sweetheart?" Rael said as he crouched down to speak to her.

"Nina," answered the girl. "Are you going to hurt my grandpa?"

"Well, Nina, here is the thing. Your grandpa has a secret, but he doesn't want to share it with me. You like secrets?"

Nina nodded slowly. Rael looked at the sensei as he spoke.

"Well, if grandpa tells me his secret I promise to let him go. How old are you, Nina?"

"Four."

"Do you like ice cream? I love ice cream. Do you want to get some while grandpa plays with my friends?"

At the mention of ice cream, Nina's face lit up with expectation. Rael stood up and spoke to the Gyrevex.

"He has information I need. Extract it."

The sensei took a step forward. The three Gyrevex turned to the sensei. Rael spoke without turning.

"I wouldn't. Innocent eyes shouldn't have to see bloodshed. Don't you agree, sensei?"

The sensei stood still. The three Gyrevex remained facing the sensei, their attention fixed.

"All you had to do was tell me. You caused this, remember that. Let's go, Nina. Do you like chocolate?" Nina grabbed Rael's hand as they left the dojo. The Gyrevex fanned out and began to spin their metal spheres.

"Very well, then," said the sensei. "A life for a life."

The sensei opened his fans with a flick. The metallic sound echoed through the dojo over the whirr of the spinning spheres. The sensei focused his chi and his fans flared bright silver. The first Gyrevex let his sphere go. The sensei twisted his body sideways. The sphere, called a bell flew past him. He immediately bent forwards to avoid the second bell that came from behind. The third Gyrevex stayed back, observing. With a tug, both Gyrevex pulled their bells back. *I need to get rid of these bells,* thought the sensei. The first Gyrevex was spinning his bell overhead, while the second spun his to the side of his body. They attacked simultaneously. The first aimed for his head, while the second came in low trying to break his legs. The sensei leapt into the air, avoiding both attacks. The third Gyrevex attacked then, sending his bell directly at the sensei. Too late, the sensei realized the tactic. He brought up his fans to shield his body from the bell. The bell struck his chest. The force of its impact was dispersed by his fans. *Two, maybe three ribs broken,* he thought as he was flung back across the dojo floor. He stood slowly as they closed on him. The first attacked, sending his bell straight at the sensei. The sensei turned around the attack, allowing the bell to pass behind him before he brought his fan down and severed the chain. The bell continued its trajectory and smashed into a wall, cratering it. Blood trickled from the sensei's mouth. He wiped it away using his sleeve. *Have to end this quickly,* he thought. He closed the distance on the first Gyrevex, who stood momentarily confused at the loss of his bell. It was all the time he needed. His fans a blur, the sensei attacked. The Gyrevex fell, dead before hitting the ground. He sensed the second bell before he saw it. Closing a fan and tucking it into his top he slid back, narrowly avoiding the attack. As it reached the end of its chain, he grabbed hold and sliced through. He let the bell fall several feet before rotating his body and returning it to its owner. It hit the Gyrevex with a sickening crunch. *One more,* he thought as a bell crashed into his side. Moments later the dojo door opened.

*****

Rael walked in to see the sensei on the floor. The last Gyrevex towered over him, spinning his bell.

"Stop. I told you I needed information from him." The Gyrevex stepped back, the bell disappearing.

"Unstoppable, but not too bright." Rael looked around the dojo and took in the scene. "Seems like I needed three after all," he said.

He crouched down near the sensei. The damage was extensive and he cursed under his breath.

"Where is Dante, sensei? Where is the weapon bearer?"

The sensei, barely conscious, looked at Rael.

"Nina."

"A life for a life, sensei. No harm will come to her if you tell me, on my word."

The sensei sighed and closed his eyes. *Too late, the old man is gone, goddammit*, thought Rael. He stood with venom in his eyes and looked at the last Gyrevex, who stood impassively to the side.

"Rael…" whispered the sensei.

Rael turned back to the broken body of the man he once knew as his teacher.

"On your word…"

"She will be safe until she comes of age and into her abilities, on my word. Where is he?" *Lucius is going to kill me for this*, he thought.

"The records, the Akashic Records," said the sensei. Moments later the sensei breathed his last. Rael stood looking at the Gyrevex.

"Well, damn. I'm going to need more than three of you to get in there. Let's go, we have a warrior to kill," he said as he walked to the exit. The Gyrevex trailed close behind.

Rael left the dojo and his past behind him.

TWO

"HE'S COMING TO," SAID a voice behind me.

For a moment all I could see was the hammer coming down over and over. Everything was blurry, and then a face came into focus: Meja.

"I thought we lost you," she said.

"Where are we?" I asked as I looked around at the group. Closest to me was Meja. Standing behind her were Zen and Kal. To the side stood Sylk and Samir looking over what appeared to be a map. Beside Sylk stood Mara at guard as usual.

"What do you mean where are we? We just arrived at the Akashic Records. Where do you think we are?"

"Devin, I saw Devin." *Did I dream that? It was too real,* I thought.

She grabbed my hand. "Devin? How did you see him? You never left my side," she said.

"I did. We were attacked by someone named Roman. He had a huge hammer," I said.

"Did you say Roman?" It was Sylk.

"Yes, I saw him attack Devin." *I don't want to say he killed him. Can anyone survive that many blows?*

"He mentioned someone named Aurora and kept saying something about how the ascendants were in danger," I said.

11

Sylk looked apprehensive.

"If Aurora is involved we have attracted the wrong kind of attention," he said.

"Who is she?" I asked. I was still shaken up from my trip. Sylk turned to face Samir.

"Not now—we don't have time. Samir, did you find it?"

"I found it," said Samir. "Extricating it will be another matter entirely."

"Leave that to me. We must make haste. Time is our enemy now. Guardian, gather up the warrior. Everyone else stay close. The Records are more treacherous than they seem."

I tried to stand and found my legs unresponsive. Sylk stood over me.

"It can be an effect of a prolonged wave-ride," said Sylk. "An unforeseen detour can sometimes cause shorts in the electrical system of the brain. You just need some time to adjust. Unfortunately, time is the one thing we have precious little of.

Sylk turned to Meja. "My sympathies, monitor. If Devin was facing Aurora's enforcer, his was a path destined to end. No one has defeated Roman's infernal hammer."

Meja, her eyes wet, turned away. "We'd better get moving, then," she said thickly.

"Guardian, if you would be so kind," said Sylk. "We need to make haste."

Zen picked me up like a sack of potatoes and placed me over his shoulder.

"You okay, Dante?" Zen asked.

I couldn't answer him. Devin had sacrificed himself for me. The image of Roman's attack kept replaying in my head. How could I be a Warrior of the Way if I couldn't keep them safe? I looked at Meja, her pain piercing my own. Before us lay the entrance to the Akashic Records and the key to ending this. The master syllabist text held the answers I needed to control Maelstrom and face Lucius. I promised myself I would stop Lucius and keep my world safe. Even if it cost me everything.

Deep within me, I heard a laugh. It was Maelstrom.

Let's see what it will take to keep that promise, vessel.

Sylk pushed open the door that led to an immense polished marble hallway. It was reminiscent of ancient Greek architecture with vaulted ceilings and large columns spaced along the hallway.

"What are these Akashic Records?" asked Zen as he looked around in wonder.

"This hallway will lead us there," said Sylk. "The Records are the repository of all knowledge."

"All knowledge, really?" said Zen. "How is that even possible?"

"Yes, really. All knowledge is stored here, if I can even use the term 'here'," said Sylk.

The feeling was coming back into my legs, an extreme version of pins and needles. I grunted in pain as Zen put me down.

"What?" asked Zen.

"Feeling's coming back," I answered as I walked around.

"Are we in the mirror? Is this another plane?" I asked.

"Yes and no," said Sylk. "The Records don't exist in any fixed point in space or time. This place"— he swept his arm around—"is merely a construct, a placeholder, something to keep our minds from snapping at the vastness of information.

"So this is all an illusion?" I placed a hand on the very real- feeling columns that towered above us.

"No, it exists like my location in the mirror. It is in-between."

Sylk turned to Samir who was looking at a map. The diagram on the map shifted and wavered.

"Where is it?" asked Sylk.

Samir pointed to a location on the map he held. "There, through that area for the next few hours."

Sylk grimaced. "Of course it would be there. Anything else would be easy," he said.

Meja stepped over to Samir and looked at the map.

"What's wrong? Where is this place?" she said.

Sylk turned to her. "To understand that is to understand the records itself. In this manifestation, we cannot just access any information. Some information, for example knowledge of future events, is beyond us," he said.

"Is that where this is?" she asked.

"No, the syllabist master text we need has been lost for centuries, which makes it part of the past. The difficulty arose when we arrived here seeking it. By doing so we altered its state and made it part of the present of this place."

"And that means?"

"As part of the present, the eternal now, so to speak, it falls under the dominion of Raja, the records keeper," said Sylk.

"What, like a librarian?" asked Zen.

Samir put the map away, folding it neatly and carefully storing it in his pocket.

"Not merely a librarian," said Samir. "Raja is a formidable deterrent for anyone who would attempt to remove information without being granted permission to do so."

"So what is this Raja, a beast?" said Zen. We can handle this."

Samir tightened his lips. "It is clear you do not understand, Guardian."

"That…is very clear indeed," said a voice from behind them. The voice was like gravel and sandpaper, and carried through the hallway with ease. Everyone turned to face the direction of the voice.

"This is Raja," said Sylk.

Dressed in a charcoal grey suit, Raja looked like an older executive on his way to the office. His bronze skin contrasted with his white shirt, which was unbuttoned at the top. It gave him an air of casualness. His black hair, shot through with streaks of grey, was trimmed short. Ice blue eyes gleamed from behind silver rimmed glasses, which he pushed up the bridge of his nose.

I noticed that something was not what it appeared and was about to use my inner sight.

"No," said Raja. His voice was laced with steel. "I strongly urge you to reconsider that course of action, warrior."

The group turned to look at me.

"I just wanted to take a closer look," I said.

"Using your inner sight on me would cause that delicate organ you call a brain much harm, resulting in what you call a psychotic break, splintering your mind. A condition I am certain you do not desire."

"You can use your inner sight?" asked Zen.

"Yes, can't you?"

Zen remained silent but shook his head as he looked at me with disbelief.

"What?" I asked.

"The acquisition and use of the inner sight takes approximately fifty to sixty years of a warrior's life," said Raja. "Since you are not close to that chronological age, your ability to do so is an anomaly. Hence the surprise from your companions."

I looked around, confirming Raja's words. Even Sylk looked somewhat surprised.

"Fine then, no inner sight. Who are you in relation to this place?" I asked.

"I am not a 'who' but a 'what'. I, like this place you stand in, am an embodiment to facilitate your use of the records. I am information manifest."

"You know everything?" asked Kal.

Raja turned to face Kal. "No, Kalysta, I am not omniscient, even though the amount of knowledge I do possess surpasses all of yours by several orders of magnitude. I am the eternal present, and as such, future events are beyond my sphere of influence."

Samir cleared his throat and stepped forward. His voice trembled slightly as he spoke. "We seek the tome of language, the master syllabist text."

"To what purpose, syllabist?"

"I must instruct the warrior in the use of the words of power, in order to restore balance and prevent the undoing of our plane."

Raja stood still a moment as if considering Samir's words.

"This is an acceptable request," said Raja.

Samir exhaled slowly.

"There is, however, one condition," said Raja.

"Yes?" said Samir as he winced.

"Once balance is restored, the warrior must spend one cycle with me."

"How long is a cycle?" asked Zen.

"Ten years according to your time," said Raja.

"Ten years!" shouted Zen. Sylk looked at him and he calmed down.

"This is Dante's choice," Sylk said. "We all will pay a price, some more than others." Sylk looked at his arm.

"Are these terms acceptable to you, warrior?" said Raja.

I didn't look forward to spending ten years with Raja in this place.

"Do the years have to be spent consecutively?" I asked. Maybe I could stretch this out over time.

"A valid question and the answer is yes. It is to be ten years sequentially given in exchange for the master syllabist text."

I took some time to consider everything that was at stake. If I didn't get that text I wouldn't be able to control Maelstrom. Ascendants would be killed, and I wouldn't be able to stop Lucius from taking over and destroying everything. Ten years seemed like a small price to pay.

"Yes, I accept this condition," I said.

"Very well. Once balance is restored and your plane is no longer under threat, you will be brought here," said Raja with finality.

Raja turned and walked down the hallway, his passage silent. He led the group to a very large door. Around the edge of the door were inscriptions that were foreign to me. I turned to Sylk and pointed.

"What do these symbols mean?"

He shook his head. "These symbols are beyond me."

"Through this door lies the text you seek. Only the warrior can enter. If he is found worthy, he will return."

"Found worthy by whom?" said Sylk. I could tell Sylk wasn't pleased by this turn of events.

Raja stood still for another moment before answering.

"You have other matters to be concerned with," said Raja as he pointed down the hallway. In the distance stood four figures and they were walking toward us.

"Dante, I think you'd better go get that book," said Zen. "We will handle this." I stepped to the door and grabbed the handle. Rather than open, I felt myself being pulled in until everything was black.

THREE

I FLOATED FOR WHAT FELT LIKE an eternity until I landed on what seemed to be solid ground. In the distance I could see some light and headed in that direction.

So you would give ten years of your life to this being? It was Maelstrom.

If it means getting this book and learning to use you without sacrificing myself in the process, ten years is a bargain, I thought.

You do know I could teach you, vessel.

Thanks for the offer, but I'll pass.

Perhaps in this place you can find out how to remove me, vessel. Think of it, no need for a book or risking your companions. Who knows what dangers they are facing right now, because of you. You know my words are sound.

No, we are getting this book to confront a greater threat. This isn't about you and me.

Naïve little vessel, of course it is. You just haven't realized it yet.

Before me stood another door. It was glowing in the dark, a soft hue of blues and greens. It stood there in the middle of the space I was in, not exactly inviting. I turned the handle, half expecting it to explode, and found myself in an immense library. Books covered each of the walls as far as I could see. Skylights were spaced along the ceiling and allowed a soft light to fall upon the books. I turned and took in the entire space. The rows seemed endless.

"Pretty impressive, isn't it?" I recognized the voice. It was my own and yet it was subtly different. Maelstrom.

I turned and saw an older version of myself sitting at a table with two books on it. He was dressed in a black cloak with red motifs. I looked closer and realized that the symbols were the inscriptions on the staff I wielded.

"Hello, Dante. You are here for this, I assume," said Maelstrom. He placed his hand on an ornate book no larger than a paperback. From the writing on it that I could see, it was the master syllabist text.

"You," I said.

"Yes, me. I'm the older, wiser version of you. The one that thinks this is a fool's errand. I am the one tempered by time who knows that I should be looking for another book, perhaps this one?"

His hand rested on the other book on the table, roughly the same size and just as ornate.

"This book will rid you of that nasty voice inside your head. You know the one that keeps telling you to kill, destroy and maim others all in an effort to shorten your life. That way you and I can both be free."

"I can't," I said.

"Can't or won't? It's not complicated, Dante. You free yourself from the weapon and there go all your problems. Let someone else handle this world-saving business. You don't need the stress."

He sat back in his chair and crossed his arms as he looked at me.

"Don't you want to be free?" he said. "You don't deserve any of this. You didn't ask for it— it was thrust upon you, unfairly I might add."

"I'm a warrior."

Maelstrom laughed.

"Don't tell me you bought into that fairytale. Wake up, Dante!" He slammed his hand on the table, startling me.

"I am awake. People need me. My world needs me," I said, my voice lacking the conviction I felt in my heart.

"Do they need *you*? *You* the coward? *You* let Devin die for you. You who can't control his weapon? They need the you that is a menace to everyone and everything around him? You're a failure before you've even begun. You're pathetic," he said.

He pushed back from the table and stood. The library disappeared and we stood in an open field.

"It seems like words alone won't do this. Very well, I will show you how unnecessary you are."

A black blade materialized in his hand.

"Time to end this, Dante."

FOUR

THE DOOR CLOSED WITH A whisper behind Dante. Sylk turned to face the group approaching. As they drew closer, his face grew dark.

"What is it?" asked Mara, concern in her voice as she drew closer to Sylk.

"Those are Gyrevex, and the one leading them is…"

"Rael," whispered Meja.

Sylk looked at Meja for a brief second.

"He is known as the Harbinger. You know him?" asked Sylk.

Meja nodded, her face grim.

"Blood Sylk, so good to see you again," Rael said as he bowed. "Meja, you are keeping strange company these days."

Meja manifested her sword, saying nothing.

"I see. Still beautiful and angry," said Rael as he turned to Sylk.

As Sylk turned to face Rael, under his cloak his right arm glowed faintly.

"Harbinger, you are not welcome here." *If he is here, it's only a matter of time before his master is free. If that happens, we have lost it all,* thought Sylk. "How many did you kill to arrive here?"

"Who's keeping track? You of all people know how that is," said Rael.

"Those days have passed," said Sylk.

"Come now, it wasn't that long ago, was it? You forgot how you earned your name, Blood Sylk."

"How? How did you manage it?" Sylk insisted.

"Enough ascendants die and the barrier grows weaker. I'm here to make sure it's weak enough for him to get through," said Rael.

"Consider your actions, Rael. You don't have to do this. He will destroy us all, including you," said Sylk in a measured tone.

"What makes you think I have a choice? Now, where is he? Where is the weapon bearer?"

"He is undergoing a trial, which must be completed," said Sylk.

"Irrelevant. My task is to bring back the weapon bearer, alive. The rest of you" —he motioned with a hand—"are obstacles to be removed. Kill them, but leave the old one alive. Him, I want to speak to," said Rael as he pointed to Sylk.

Raja stood off to the side observing as the Gyrevex began spinning their bells. Everyone except Raja backed away.

"What the hell are those things?" said Zen.

"Gyrevex, and the bells they are spinning weigh close to fifty pounds," said Sylk. "They are chi weapons. Don't let them hit you."

"You forgot the part where you describe their unstoppable nature, how they don't feel pain and are almost impossible to kill," said Rael.

"We can do this without needless bloodshed, Rael," said Sylk.

Rael held up his hand and the Gyrevex stopped spinning the bells.

"I'm listening," said Rael.

"You defeat me and you can have the warrior. If I best you we leave here with safe passage," Sylk said.

Rael remained silent a moment before a smile crept onto his face.

"If you beat me, I will allow you safe passage. When I defeat you I will take the warrior and maybe let my friends play with yours. If they try and save you or interfere in any way, I unleash them," he said pointing to the Gyrevex. "Do we understand each other?"

"Perfectly," said Sylk as he threw off his cloak and manifested his blade.

Rael drew his swords as Sylk approached, energy coursing through the blades.

"The last time we did this it didn't go so well for you," said Rael.

"That was a long time ago. I have learned a few things since then."

Sylk sent his chi down into his sword and caused it to turn transparent. Around him small orbs materialized, circling his body.

"Why fight the inevitable? You know my master will triumph in the end. Don't throw your life away. Join us," said Rael.

Behind them the group had moved to the periphery of the hallway. Mara stepped over to Raja.

"Are you going to let them fight, in here?"

"Yes, regardless of the outcome, what Dante has begun must run its course. Whether he survives it has no bearing on this conflict," said Raja.

"And if the Harbinger wins?" said Mara.

"That would be most unfortunate for your lord, I think."

Mara remained silent.

FIVE

"THIS WILL BE OVER QUICKLY, vessel."

We were in an open field and he began circling me. It was ironic that at that moment I almost called on Maelstrom, but I felt empty. Even if I tried I knew what would happen.

He smiled at me then.

In that moment I remembered I wasn't completely unarmed. I reached into my side for the hard rectangle, Mariko's fan. I didn't know how to use it properly, but anything was better than going up

27

against him empty-handed. The black blade in his hand gave off wisps of dark energy. I knew I didn't want to be cut by it.

Don't give in to the fear, Dante.

It was Owl.

Easy to say, not so easy to do, Samadhi.

If you give in to the fear, then you will lose yourself.

How can I fight him? I have no weapon except this fan.

You are a warrior of the way. The weapon does not make the warrior, it is the warrior that makes the weapon.

With those words Owl was gone. I no longer sensed his presence. Maelstrom came at me then. I managed to parry the first thrust on instinct alone. Mariko's fan was a lot stronger than it appeared. Something Owl said nagged at me, but dodging a sword intending on splitting me in two kept me from giving it much thought. I stayed out of reach as he circled me.

"You can't hope to defeat me with a fan," he said.

I didn't answer, not trusting my voice. He was right— I was no match for him. No, that was the fear talking.

"What happened to our truce?" I asked as we circled each other.

"You are weak and a coward. I would rather roam the void than remain within such a vessel," he said.

He slashed downward at my legs, a feint. Using the fan I blocked the slash and drove a palm heel at his solar plexus before he could execute the real attack, an upward strike meant to disembowel me. My strike unbalanced him, but he recovered instantly. He brushed the front of his cloak with his free hand.

"Why use a sword? Why not a jo?" I asked.

"Good question. Remind me to answer you as you lay dying," he said as he lunged.

I backpedaled as the sword sliced through my shirt, cutting me on the left side. He pressed his advantage, slamming the side of my head with a back fist. My vision exploded with light. A series of punches followed and I knew he was toying with me. In the midst of the pain and helplessness, Owl's words came back to me. *It's not the weapon that makes the warrior. It's the warrior that makes the weapon.* I make the weapon. Then it dawned on me. I rolled back away from the flurry of blows and directed my chi inward, calling Maelstrom. In my hands materialized my weapon, white and golden. I understood now. I was facing my darker self, the part of me Maelstrom wanted.

"That won't help you," he said.

"You mean it won't help *you*," I said as I ran toward him.

I slammed my jo down, intending to crush his skull. He brought up his sword in time to stop my attack, but left himself open to my secondary and real attack. With our weapons locked, I flicked open Mariko's fan and sliced across his neck. Its razor sharp edge cut through him with ease. He fell back, grabbing his neck, but I saw no blood. He fell to the ground and disappeared along with my weapon as I found myself in the library again. Two books sat on the table before me.

"Choose wisely, warrior. Even now your companions face death," said Raja as he materialized beside me.

"What do you mean?"

"You can save them by removing the weapon, thus rendering you a non-threat and allowing another to shoulder the burden."

"Or?"

"You can choose that book," —he pointed at the master syllabist text— "ensuring that one or all of you may die in these halls."

I grabbed the master syllabist text. It felt heavy, given the choice.

"Very well, the choice has been made," said Raja. As he slowly faded away, his voice drifted over to me. "Prepare yourself ,warrior."

The library filled with a fog and in a few moments all I could see was the nebulous white all around me.

Several feet in front of me I thought I saw the outline of a door. I headed in that direction and found myself before the same door that led me here. I turned the handle and felt that same pulling sensation. Then everything went black.

SIX

I FELT LIKE I WAS BEING STRETCHED in every direction. Then in a moment every sense felt heightened and I snapped back, finding myself in the hallway. Sylk, sword drawn and surrounded by flying orbs, was squaring off with a swordsman with two blades. The swordsman looked experienced. I could see in his movements and posture that fighting was a way of life for him. There was an edge to his voice, sharper than any sword.

"Dante, so good of you to join us," he said, never taking his eyes off Sylk.

"Do I know you?"

"I am the Harbinger. You have something that belongs to my master. I need it back," he said.

The next moment Maelstrom was in my hands, gleaming white and golden.

"No!" yelled Sylk as Rael turned and signaled to the Gyrevex.

"Get the weapon. Kill everyone. Sorry, old man, orders are orders."

31

Sylk sent the orbs flying at Rael as the three giants headed my way.

"Don't let them get that weapon," yelled Sylk. "Keep Dante safe. Go!"

The rest of the group ran behind the giants as Sylk faced the Harbinger. I felt the vibration travel along the floor as they approached. In their hands, large kettle bells attached to thick chains swung with each step.

Do not allow the bells to touch you-, Owl whispered in my mind.

That was the plan. Can I face these things? I thought as I headed toward the trio. Maelstrom pulsed in my hands.

Not alone, do not take the Gyrevex lightly.

The Gyrevex started spinning their bells as they drew closer. The whirr of displaced air held a quiet menace. I realized that the group would be too late to intervene in the first attack. *So much for not taking them on alone,* I thought as the first bell came at me. I held up Maelstrom half expecting the bell to shatter it on impact. As the bell hit, the buildup of energy was immediate. I could feel the surge within Maelstrom as it absorbed the blow. *Those are chi weapons?* I looked around for the others but couldn't see past my attacker. Another bell sailed past me, just missing my head as the second Gyrevex converged on me. Things were getting bad in a hurry.

"I got your back, Dante," said a familiar voice behind me—Zen.

"I can't take these things on alone, Zen," I said.

I didn't know how he got behind me, but I was glad he was there.

"You don't have to," he said.

He concentrated a moment and I saw his halberd materialize in his hands. Meja and Kal managed to intercept the third Gyrevex, which left two for me and Zen. All around me all I could sense was motion.

You must see without your eyes, Owl whispered.

I took a deep breath and deliberately sent my chi inward, slowing everything down. In the space of a breath I could see what I needed to do.

"Back me up here," I told Zen as I stepped closer to the Gyrevex nearest me.

Zen, who towered above me, was dwarfed by these giants. I could take it all in. Sylk was facing the Harbinger. Mara was drawing closer to Sylk. Meja and Kal were dodging the bell from the third Gyrevex, looking for an opening. Samir and Raja stood off to the side away from the deadly exchanges. A bell came at my chest. I could sense the displaced air as it rushed toward me. At the last second I slid to the side, exposing Zen who stood behind me. As the bell reached the end of its chain, Zen let it wrap itself around his weapon and then tugged using the momentum of the bell. The Gyrevex was larger, but Zen had leverage on his side as he pulled. The Gyrevex lost his footing and stumbled forward.

"*Devolver*," I whispered and touched the bell with Maelstrom. It was instantly absorbed into my weapon. I half expected another bell to form in the Gyrevex's hands but it fell forward, landing on all fours, a surprised look on its face. Zen sent his halberd through its back, dispatching it. The second Gyrevex caught me with a back hand that sent me sailing as the world exploded in a bright light. I turned in time to see Zen take a bell to the leg and heard the sickening crunch of metal on flesh. I was still off balance when I heard the whirr of the bell. I wasn't going to be able to dodge this next attack. I couldn't even see where the bell was.

As long as I hear that whirr it means it's not coming at me, I thought. It was a small consolation. Behind me and to the side I could hear Zen grunt in pain as he tried to move into position for an attack. I took a few steps and the floor tilted. *Everyone is going to die here unless I can get it together.* The word came to me then. It was the word I had used when I last fought Owl. If I used it I could eliminate the Gyrevex. I didn't know what it would do to Rael. He seemed almost as powerful as Sylk. There was only one downside: if I used it, it would kill everyone around me. The Gyrevex were after me, after Maelstrom. I let my anger take over and slowly the weapon turned from white and gold to black and crimson.

"This is what you want. Come and get it," I said. The remaining two Gyrevex shifted and ran toward me.

"Meja, get them safe!" I yelled. The word was already forming on my lips when Samir covered my mouth.

"Please, warrior, do not say something you will regret," he whispered. "In this place every word of power you use is magnified." He placed a hand on Maelstrom as the Gyrevex bore down on us. "Tempus repit," he said as everything crawled to a standstill.

"What did you do?" I said.

"I have bought us seconds only, long enough for us to be away," said Samir.

I was stunned. Samir had slowed time. "How? How did you manage this?"

"If you could do this why not do it from the beginning?" I said.

"This is not my doing alone. He helped," Samir said as he looked at Raja.

I turned to see that Raja had not been affected by the words of power. He gave me a slight nod as if to say-*remember our agreement.* Samir shook me by the shoulder, fear clear in his eyes.

"Focus, warrior! Fix us in your mind. You will only be able to take three with you. Say with me: *regreseo.*"

It meant I would have to leave three of them behind. I needed to take Zen since he was injured. Meja could get us back, I hoped, and Samir knew the words I needed. It would mean leaving Sylk, Mara and Kalysta. I couldn't do this. He must have seen the reluctance on my face.

"You must do this, warrior. If they get you and the weapon, all is lost," he said.

I knew he was right. I closed my eyes as time began to resume its normal flow. I could feel Samir's hand clench my arm. The vibrations of the Gyrevex resumed as they closed on us.

"Warrior…" Samir's voice rose with fear.

"*Regreseo,*" I said and the world faded away.

SEVEN

SYLK SENSED THEIR ABSENCE the next moment and smiled. He could see Mara going to assist Kal with the Gyrevex she was now facing alone. Avoiding a slash and stepping back from a lunge, he put distance between himself and Rael. He needed to know how they were followed.

"Give it up, Harbinger," said Sylk. "He is gone. Even I don't know where they are."

"How did you think I found him here, of all places?" said Rael.

Sylk remained silent a moment and then it hit him.

"The weapon, you are tracking the weapon."

"There is nowhere, no plane where your warrior goes that I can't find him, eventually," Rael said as the energy coursed through his swords.

Sylk surrounded himself with orbs as Rael attacked. The orbs coalesced to form a shield, stopping one of the swords as he parried the other with his own sword.

"You've grown stronger, old man. It's good to see you haven't wasted your time all these years," said Rael, sidestepping the shield and lunging at Sylk. As Sylk turned, allowing the lunge to go past, he traced symbols with his right arm, leaving a silver trail behind him.

"All the pretty symbols in the world aren't going to save you now."

"I don't need them to save me, I just need them to hold you in place," said Sylk. In moments the marble beneath Rael liquefied and he sank into the floor. Sylk took advantage of the distraction to press his attack, getting past Rael's defense and driving his sword through his midsection. Rael doubled over, grasping the wound. Sylk backed up slowly as the ground solidified around Rael. Then Rael began laughing, chilling Sylk to the bone.

"You still don't understand, Blood Sylk," said Rael. "I am the Harbinger. You are going to have to do more than stab me with your sword, if you plan on stopping me."

Rael thrust both swords into the marble around his feet and began channeling energy downwards. In moments he would be free of the trap Sylk set.

"I didn't think that would end you. I just needed you to be still while I did this," said Sylk as he ran over and grabbed Rael with his right hand. Energy began siphoning into Sylk.

"What are you doing?"

"Making sure you can't follow us for some time. It takes a large amount of energy to enter this place. It takes even more to leave. I'm guessing you have quite a bit of chi stored within you if you can keep those two going," said Sylk as he looked at the Gyrevex. As he said these words, Rael dropped to his knees.

"Clever, but that won't help you. I will find the warrior and take the weapon back."

"I may not be able to stop you, but I think he can. By the time you find us again I will make sure he is ready."

Sylk siphoned more energy as the lines in his arm began to grow bright. He stepped back, not daring to take any more. Rael looked at him with a sad smile.

Behind them, the Gyrevex stopped moving and fell forward, immobile.

"You can't kill me—no one can. Do you know how many times I have wished it? Each time I thought it was the end, he brought me back. This is the price of my betrayal," said Rael.

"That was the path you chose, Rael," said Sylk.

Mara and Kal came up behind Sylk. Rael began to grow incorporeal.

"Enjoy this small victory, since when we meet next I can assure you the outcome will be different," said Rael, and he disappeared.

"Did you—?" began Mara.

"No, he isn't that easy to kill. I just made it very hard for him to remain in that form," said Sylk.

Mara and Kal were both bruised from their fight with the Gyrevex.

"Can you kill him? He looked like one of those 'make sure you kill and scatter the ashes' types," said Kal.

"I don't think I can. With all the energy I siphoned from him, he was still present. It would have been enough to end anyone else."

Sylk looked down at his arm and the energy coursing through it. "I have to expend this energy before it does more damage than good."

"Where did they go?" asked Mara.

"I don't know, but I do have an idea who does," said Sylk as he looked at Raja.

EIGHT

ZEN GRUNTED IN PAIN WHEN we arrived. His leg was broken.

"What did you do, Dante?" asked Meja.

"I got us out of danger," I said.

"No, you gave them a death sentence. Did you stop to think what would happen to them?" She let the words hang in the air. "Rael will kill them without mercy."

"You know him?" I said.

"I knew him, before—before he became what he is now."

"And what is he now? What is the Harbinger?" I said, anger creeping into my voice.

"He serves Lucius now. He used to be a good man, a good monitor and a friend…" She didn't elaborate further, but I could tell there was something else—something more.

"And now?"

"And now it doesn't matter. He is an enemy and will be dealt with as such," she said, her words clipped.

I thought back to what had happened at the Records. At the time I hadn't stopped to think. I only wanted to get everyone out of danger. Except I didn't get everyone out.

"If they got my weapon it would be a death sentence for all of us," I said as the edge of anger rose. *Would a simple 'thank you' be too much to ask?*

She stepped close to me then. "*My* weapon? Since when is it *your* weapon? That abomination you call a weapon belongs to Lucius and will end up getting us all killed," she said.

Samir came between us, his presence a calming influence. Meja made her way over to Zen and began working on his leg.

"Where are we?" I asked Samir, anxious to change the subject of my weapon's ownership.

"The last place we were before we entered the Records. That is what that word of power does," said Samir.

I took in the courtyard and the black obelisk at its center. It was covered in symbols and I could feel the energy it was giving off.

"We are back…" I began.

"In the South Watch," said a voice. We all turned to face the Keeper. Beside him stood one of the Rah Ven, a Watch guardian. Dwarfing most wolves by several feet, it padded over silently to a spot and sat, its deep yellow eyes fixed on us.

The Keeper stepped over to where Zen lay and placed a hand on his leg. A soft light travelled from his hand to the leg. Zen lost consciousness the next moment as several young men came and carried him off.

"His leg will heal. He just needs some time," said the Keeper.

Meja looked at me as they carried Zen away. "Why are we here?"

Samir spoke before I could answer. "It was I who gave him the word to speak. That word— do you remember it, warrior?" I nodded in response. "That word will return you to the last place you have been. Remember it but use it wisely. It only works once a day," he said.

The Keeper sat on a bench that materialized under him.

"My old bones need rest. I see some of your group is missing?" said the Keeper as he rested his staff beside him. A small smile played on his lips.

"We were in danger and had to leave. Someone called the 'Harbinger' attacked us while in the Records," said Samir.

"The Harbinger, did you say? Did you manage to get the text?" asked the Keeper.

Everyone looked at me as I checked the inside of my cloak and pulled out the small book the size of a paperback. The cover was dark leather and the pages were edged in gold. Each page felt fragile, as if the book would disintegrate if handled too much. I gave the book to Samir.

"The master text. I did not think I would see this in my lifetime," he said as he held the book in his open hands. "We must begin your training at once."

"What about the others?" I said.

"Yes, Samir, what about the others? Who are most likely dead by now," said Meja as she looked at me.

"You have my sympathies, monitor, but my purpose is to prepare the warrior. He must be ready when he faces the Harbinger again. We are all secondary to that purpose," Samir said, his voice low.

"Sylk and his thrall mean nothing to me, but Kal was one of mine," she said as she continued looking at me.

"The syllabist is right. There is nothing to be done in this moment. The Records will have shifted location and will not be accessible from this doorway for several days. It would be best to use that time in rest and training," said the Keeper.

Meja clenched her jaw and squeezed her hand closed until the knuckles popped.

"You can stay here and train. As soon as that doorway is open I have a monitor to find. With or without you," she said as she stalked off.

"We do not have much time, warrior," said Samir. "Let us begin." He gripped my shoulder for a moment and then headed off to another part of the Watch.

I looked back over my shoulder to see Meja heading out of the Watch into the desert.

"You do well to be concerned, warrior. Anger is a great weapon and a great weakness," said the Keeper.

I followed Samir, not knowing if those words were for Meja or for me.

NINE

"WHERE DID THEY GO?" said Mara.

Raja stood still as if accessing some information, his gaze blank and out of focus. He returned and focused his gaze on them.

"They are currently in the South Watch, which is inaccessible from here at this moment."

"What do you mean 'inaccessible'?" said Kal.

"I apologize, was I unclear? You cannot return to the South Watch from this location until the planes align again," said Raja.

Kal shot him a dark look. If Raja noticed he gave no indication.

"How long until they realign?" said Mara.

"It doesn't matter. Without the monitor, we can't get there. Only Meja knows how to locate the Watch," said Sylk.

"We are standing in the largest information center in this and any other plane, and we can't figure a way there?" asked Kal. "Are you kidding me?"

"I do not kid," said Raja. "However, there is another way to reach the Watch."

"How?" said Kal. "You have a door here that will take us there?"

"I do not, but he does," said Raja, gesturing at Sylk. "You are bound to the Watch, are you not? You can use that bond to open a pathway, in three days. When the planes align once again."

"I had not considered that to be an option," said Sylk as he looked at his arm. "The theory is sound, but I have never done it before."

"Wait. What happens if you are wrong and we can't get to the Watch?" asked Kal.

"Then there is a good chance we will be stuck in between somewhere, like Mariko," said Sylk. " I need to read on this process, Raja. Is it available?"

"What about those things?" asked Kal. She pointed at the immobile Gyrevex. "Are we going to have to deal with them again?"

"They are inert for now, at least until Rael draws enough chi to return," said Sylk.

Kal gave them a wary look.

"Please follow me. There are quarters for you to wait in until the alignment," said Raja.

"Oh great, a three-day layover in the twilight zone. This is going to be a blast," said Kal as they followed after Raja. Out of the corner of her eye she noticed the movement.

Kal grabbed Mara's arm as they were walking away.

"Did you see that?" said Kal.

"See what?"

"I swear one of those things moved," Kal said, pointing at the Gyrevex.

"They can't. Sylk removed Rael from this plane. They have no volition of their own," Mara said as she walked away after Sylk.

"I know what I saw," said Kal.

TEN

"DO NOT THINK OF THEM as words, Dante," said Samir. Rather see them as vehicles for your chi. Vessels that carry your intention."

At the mention of the word 'vessels', I cringed. It was how Maelstrom saw me.

"You do not like this analogy? I'm sorry, my English still needs polishing," said Samir.

"No, no, that was fine, I get it I think," I said and read the next word.

I extended my hand and whispered *luminare,* and a miniscule, inadequate orb of light appeared in my hand.

"There are several types of words," said Samir. "Some are fixed in their results and no amount of emotion will change the outcome of their use. There are others that are dependent on the emotion used when spoken. More emotion means more chi used, less or no emotion means minimal to no effect. Try the same word again but now with feeling."

"Luminare!" I said, louder than before.

The same orb appeared in my hand.

"I did not say louder, I said with feeling. Use your chi and let it flow through you. The word merely captures the chi that is flowing in and around you."

I gathered my breath and felt my chi flowing within. I channeled it and spoke.

"Luminare," I said. A white flash blinded me instantly.

"That was much better," said Samir as he removed a pair of sunglasses.

"A little warning would have been nice," I said as I blinked my eyes several times.

"Ah, but then you would not have appreciated the difference in intensity," he said with a smile.

"Yeah, thanks for that," I said, still seeing spots.

He handed me a short staff to match his own.

"Now that you understand intensity and intent, you must learn to use the words while under stress," he said as he turned his staff slowly.

"Do you know how to fight? I didn't think—," I started when his staff came whirling at my head. I ducked as he just missed me.

"That is good— don't think, just do," he said as he lunged at me again.

The sound of wood clashing filled the room as he pressed his attacks and I parried.

"I sense you are not fighting me, warrior," he said as he stopped attacking.

"I don't want to hurt you," I said.

"That is a noble sentiment. Please, do not hold back," he said.

He bowed and entered a fighting stance. I recognized the stance from my own training. He slid in and attacked a feint at my legs. I stepped back, sending my staff forward to stop his momentum. He executed a sharp shift at the waist and trapped my weapon with his own. It was elegant in its deception.

"You are still thinking, warrior. In the heat of battle you will not have time for this. Thought is too slow."

He handed me my staff and again assumed a fighting stance.

You want real? Fine, let's see how skilled you really are, I thought as I started my attack. I came in with a low attack that suddenly switched to mid-level. He met my staff on the rising arc as he turned his body into my 'hot side'. I expected him to go the other way and was out of position when his fist connected with my nose. My eyes teared up instantly, making it hard to see. He followed that with a palm-heel strike to my chest that sent the air out of my lungs and landed me on my ass.

"You must do better than this, warrior," he said as a small smile played on his lips. Sweat drenched us both by this time, but he seemed full of energy.

Who is this guy? I stepped in and attacked, a downward strike designed to shatter the collarbone. He parried the attack by making it glance off his staff as he crouched down. I delivered a knee kick to his midsection, which doubled him over. I followed with a staff strike to his back that he stopped, and rolling forward and to his feet, he turned to face me.

"Much better— now we are getting somewhere," he said as he launched himself at me again. He was a flurry of attack. He came in close and we locked weapons.

"Now you must use the word you have learned today in the midst of this, warrior. Use it," he said between grunts as he tried to push me back.

"Luminare," I said and then the world shook.

ELEVEN

KAL WALKED OVER TO THE INERT Gyrevex and prodded them with her boot. Nothing.

"Maybe Mara was right. I must be seeing things."

It was the whirr of the chain that saved her life. On instinct she rolled to the side, avoiding the bell that cracked the marble where she stood moments before.

"You're fast for one so young," said Rael.

He stepped out from behind one of the pillars, swords in hand.

"I thought he—I saw you disappear," stammered Kal. *Oh, shit.*

"Sylk was always a bit on the arrogant side. I just showed him what he wanted to see," he said.

Kal drew her sword knowing it was a futile gesture.

"You, however, have seen more than you should have. I want him to think I am gone. I can't have you telling him I'm still here," he said as he sheathed his swords.

"So, you surrender? Smart move, I would hate to have to kick your ass," she said.

He laughed at her as he walked away as one of the Gyrevex trailed behind him. "I don't think so," he said turning to the remaining Gyrevex. "Kill her and then catch up to me."

The Gyrevex approached, bell spinning. Kal felt the sweat running down her back. *I wish Val were here, she'd tell me to bring my A game and stop this thing,* Kal thought.

"Fine, let's dance, then," she said as she channeled chi into her sword.

The bell came at her, the intent clear. She dropped back to the floor and rolled to the side, avoiding another smashing blow by inches. Every time she tried to get close the Gyrevex would pivot and send the bell at her. It forced her to dodge attack after attack. *I can't keep doing this,* she thought.

What she lacked in size and strength she made up for in speed and agility. *I need to get closer, inside the circle.* She drew a small blade and leapt at the Gyrevex, twisting mid-air to avoid a bell strike. She landed beside the Gyrevex, exactly where she wanted to be. Working her way up from the bottom she began slashing at the vulnerable points of the Gyrevex. She slashed the calves and then the knees and ducked under the haymaker that would have caved in her skull had it connected. She rolled back and stepped to the side and rolled back in. The Gyrevex was waiting for her and kicked her in the side, sending her sprawling. She managed to get her arm down in time to deflect the impact of the kick, grunting as the kick just missed her ribs. *Damn it's fast. Thing hits like a truck— don't want to do that again. Think Kal or it's over.*

She channeled her chi inward, giving her the ability to heighten her reflexes. The Gyrevex unleashed another attack, sending the bell at her head. She leapt straight up, timing the release of the bell to miss her by a fraction of an inch. At the top of her jump she threw her dagger, burying it in the Gyrevex's eye and blinding it. If it felt pain it didn't show it. It pulled out the dagger and tossed it to one side. It moved its head left and right to find her. Once it saw her it roared, a scream of anger and frustration. The sound chilled Kal to her core.

The bell disappeared in the Gyrevex's hand and it charged at her. She stood still and materialized two daggers as her sword disappeared. This was what she wanted. She wanted it close and furious. It was where she lived inside the circle, the circle of death. The Gyrevex lunged at her. She slashed down, cutting the hand. Spinning around the giant she buried a blade in its chest, but it didn't even slow. A fist crashed into her midsection as it grabbed her hair with the other hand. She cut above her, leaving it with a handful of her hair. It reached with the other hand to grab her arm. She ducked under the grab and stabbed into the armpit of the extended arm. The Gyrevex took a step back and then spun with its arm extended, the blow catching her and sending her across the floor. She managed to roll out of the fall only to see the Gyrevex charging at her again. She jumped back and avoided a stomp that would have broken her leg. Attacking from the blind side, she lunged at the Gyrevex, tucking her legs in under her to change trajectory mid-flight. Landing on its chest she buried both daggers in its neck. The Gyrevex reached up and grabbed her by the neck and squeezed. She snapped its thumb and fell to the floor as it took several steps toward her before falling as well.

Goddamnit, these things don't quit. Glad it was only one, she thought as the Gyrevex lay still. She took stock of her injuries. *At least one—no, two ribs cracked. Knee is twisted and wrist hurts like hell, but I'm still here, Val. I'm not done yet, s*he thought before she passed out.

Mara came rushing in to the hallway and saw Kal's battered body slumped against one of the columns. The body of the Gyrevex lay next to her, lifeless.

"Kal, what did this?" she said, more to herself than to Kal. She looked around and saw that one of the Gyrevex was missing. "Impossible, but that would mean…" She never finished her sentence as she looked down to see the sword protruding from her chest. She fell off the blade to the ground beside Kal.

"It would mean that I'm still around," said Rael as he wiped his sword.

He buried his swords in the body of the Gyrevex on the floor and absorbed the energy, causing it disintegrate.

"Never good to waste. Let's go, the weapon bearer is at the South Watch," said Rael as he opened a portal leaving the Records behind.

"Do you think he believed it?" said Mara as her duplicate on the ground vanished.

"We showed him what he wanted to see and now we know just how powerful he has become," said Sylk. "Please tend to the monitor. Meja would never forgive me if more harm came to her."

Mara began tending to Kal's injuries. "It would be better if we could move her somewhere else."

"I know just the place," said Sylk.

TWELVE

I WAS STILL SEEING SPOTS from the word of power when Rin appeared.

"We are under attack!" he yelled.

"Where is the Keeper?" I asked.

"He is dealing with the attackers. He instructed me to find you and to escort you out of the Watch. It would seem others are alerted to your presence here. You were asked for by name," said Rin.

"Rael," I said.

We were running toward one of the inner rooms, away from the fighting.

"Where are we going? Take me to the fighting," I said, pulling Rin's arms and stopping him short. He turned quickly and escaped my grasp while twisting in a circular fashion and trapping my arm.

"Sorry, reflex," he said as he let me my arm go.

"No problem, but why aren't we going to the fighting? I can help," I said.

"You are going to help the Keeper and the Rah Ven?" said Rin, "Forgive me if I offend, but I don't think your abilities are required."

"If someone is crazy enough to attack a Watch, you want me there, where the fighting is."

"I was instructed to get you out of the Watch, not put you in danger," said Rin.

"Zen is in there," I said.

"We will keep him safe, you have my word," said Rin.

Samir nodded. "This is the wisest course. We must keep you away from the Harbinger at all costs. You are not ready to face him."

"This is insane, if the Watch is in trouble then they need my help," I said.

Samir grabbed my arm and pulled me to the side as Rin began preparing a doorway out of the Watch. I could see him tracing symbols in the air and red trails of light following his hands.

"Are you sure it would be help? What if you or your weapon fell into their hands?" He had a point, even though I didn't want to admit it.

"I won't let them have it," I said.

"Better not to give them the option," said Samir.

"The monitor will be here shortly. Another was instructed to bring her here," said Rin. He finished tracing the symbols when two figures came running our way. One I recognized, Meja. The other I couldn't place.

"Who is that?" I asked Rin.

"Ah, that is your guide. She is Rah Ven. Her name is Luna," said Rin.

"She is what?"

"No time, she will take you through this portal. You will need her on the other side. I am sending you to the safest place imaginable."

Meja drew up short and stared at us. It seemed she was up to speed and began assisting Rin. In the distance I could hear explosions. Tremors shook the ground, again causing us to stumble.

"Where is this? Where is this safe place?" I asked.

The portal was open as the symbols traced the circular outline roughly ten feet across and just as wide.

"We are going to my home plane," said Luna as we ran in.

THIRTEEN

"THIS SHOULD SUFFICE FOR the time being," said Sylk.

"What is this place?" said Mara, looking around.

They were in a large home constructed in a traditional Japanese style. Furniture was minimal. The floors were hardwood, although some areas were covered with tatami mats. Mara could see a small shrine in the rear of the space. Most of the windows were covered with wooden slats and they were open, looking out to an open field and a small lake.

"This is one of my homes," said Sylk. "Take her upstairs, you should find everything you need to treat her injuries and make her comfortable."

"Bandages and first aid kit?" said Mara.

"Yes, a full medical kit and a safe room should you need it. Do not leave the property for any reason," he said and described the location of the safe room and how to access it.

"I thought you said this place was safe?" she said.

"Sometimes the safest place is actually the most dangerous. This place is shielded from Watchers but only as far as the house."

"What happens if I go outside? Wait, where are you going?"

Sylk remained silent as he traced the symbols for the portal to the Watch.

"Dante and the rest are at the South Watch. I'm going to try and get to him before Rael does. Going outside of the house will invite Watchers and death."

"But Raja said the doorway wasn't ready," said Mara.

"From the Records. This place is quite different. I should be able to access the Watch from here."

"What if you're wrong?"

"There is only one way to find out," he said and extended his right arm, creating a silver portal that seemed to coalesce from the energy in his arm. He fell to one knee as sweat covered his face.

"Master?" Her voice was full of concern.

"Hmm, that wasn't as painful as I thought it would be," he said through gritted teeth.

"I should return soon with the others. Remember, don't go outside," he said as he entered the shimmering portal. It lingered for a moment longer then vanished.

FOURTEEN

THE SOUTH WATCH SMOLDERED as the attack increased in intensity. Sylk arrived as a Rah Ven took down one of the attackers shredding an arm and leg only to be bisected by energy of some kind.

Who or what could wield this kind of power? He saw a pack of five Rah Ven chase down a larger group of attackers. They were dressed in what appeared to be dark blue monitor fighting garb, which belonged to the elite unit. As they entered the desert, the Rah Ven camouflaged as soon as they hit the sand, shimmering into nothingness. The screams and blood came soon after as the Rah Ven dropped their camouflage, covered in gore and blood. He ran into the courtyard unnoticed in the chaos and found Rin who was fighting two attackers at once.

"Where is the Keeper?" said Sylk as he parried an attack and plunged his sword in an attacker's throat.

"I don't know, I haven't seen him in some time," said Rin as he dodged several short thrusts from his attacker and delivered a killing blow with an elbow strike, crashing against the attacker's skull.

These aren't Gyrevex. Which means this is not the Harbinger's doing. Then who? If I didn't know better I would say they were some kind of rogue monitors, thought Sylk.

Then Sylk heard the sound.

He grabbed Rin by the shoulder, practically spinning him in place.

"You must gather all who are here and leave now. Find the Keeper if you can and get him away," said Sylk. "The Watch is lost. Save all you can. Go now!"

Rin, visibly shaken, ran off to begin the evacuation as Sylk headed deeper into the Watch. He saw as a Rah Ven leapt into the air, only to land in several parts scattered around the courtyard. All around him were scenes of death and destruction. It was clear the Watch had suffered the greater losses.

The sound came again, closer this time. Sylk had known it only as the sound of certain death. It was the sound of a muffled explosion followed by slicing wind. It was the sound of Roman's hammer unleashed.

In the center of the courtyard, beside the obelisk covered in symbols, stood the Keeper. He was bloodied, and his robe was torn in several places as he leaned on his staff. In front of the Keeper stood Roman, dressed like the attackers only in black. His jet black hair hung straight and framed his face. He had a thin but muscular frame. In his hands, he held a double-headed hammer that was almost as large as he was. Sylk stood behind a wall in direct view of the Keeper.

"Tell me where he is, Keeper," said Roman.

"You know I cannot."

"You will bear witness as I reduce this Watch to rubble?"

"Do what you must," said the Keeper. "Your mistress must know that it will not remain rubble for long."

"If you know her, then you know she does not suffer failure," said Roman. "One last time, ancient one, where is the core ascendant?"

Sylk stopped in his approach. He was certain Roman had not seen him yet. He knew the Keeper knew he was there. *Was Roman referring to Dante?*

"He is no longer on this plane. That is all I know," said the Keeper.

"Do you understand what is at stake here?" said Roman as he swung his hammer at the attacking Rah Ven. The hammer struck the ground before the Rah Ven sending a shockwave in all directions. The Keeper raised his staff to deflect the energy, but the Rah Ven, was not so lucky. The energy from the shockwave caught it full on, slicing it into smaller pieces.

"The question is, do you?" said the Keeper.

As the Keeper leaned on his staff, Sylk could see that he was barely hanging on. He was about to move out of his position when the Keeper looked at him and gave a small shake of his head.

"More riddles," said Roman. "Pathetic. Your so-called guardians are useless against me."

"They too do what they are sworn to do," said the Keeper.

"Very well, old one. My patience is at its end," said Roman as he struck the obelisk, shattering it. "Tear it down. Don't leave one brick sitting atop another," he said to several of the attackers standing behind him. They ran off in different directions at the instruction given.

"I will find him and he will do what needs to be done to keep the balance," said Roman.

"Even if it costs him his life?" said the Keeper.

"What is one life in comparison to billions?" said Roman as one of the attackers came next to him. Roman nodded as the attacker said something.

"Do it," he said to the attacker. "We continue the search until we have him."

"Each life is precious," said the Keeper.

The attacker nodded and headed off into the Watch.

"You have only prolonged the inevitable," said Roman as the walls of the Watch began to vibrate and crumble. The Keeper slowly faded as Roman opened a portal and stepped through, leaving destruction in his wake.

Sylk ran over to where he last saw the Keeper. He could sense his presence, but it was faint.

"You cannot face him alone, Karashihan," said the Keeper from behind him. Sylk turned to see the Keeper looking weary as he sat on a bench that formed itself under him. His robe was intact and the blood was gone.

"The Watch?"

"Is safe. This was not a true attack--merely a show of force. Aurora knows the Watch cannot be destroyed so easily. This structure is only a portion of the actual Watch. Most of it is underground. It does take its toll, however. So many lost today, senseless," said the Keeper.

Sylk looked around, taking in the devastation. "It has the appearance of an attack. Why didn't you let me…?"

"Roman has grown in power. More than you can imagine. It would seem that Aurora has elevated him."

"He is ascended?" said Sylk.

"No, this power is not his. It has another source."

"What source?"

"This is what you must discover, in order to defeat him."

"Where are Dante and the others?" said Sylk, looking around at the destruction and bodies strewn around the courtyard. The smell of fire and flesh filled his nostrils. He wished it were an unfamiliar scene.

"Look to Grawl of the Rah Ven, he will know," said the Keeper as he headed into what remained of the Watch.

FIFTEEN

LUNA GUIDED US THROUGH the streets of her city. It felt like any other small city. There was the bustle of activity with people going to and fro. I had a hard time imagining that every person I saw was a Rah Ven.

"This feels just like New York, only smaller," I said.

She smiled and then it faded. "This is one of the last cities of my people. We are spread out all over the planes," she said. "Once this is gone we will be on our way to becoming extinct."

"Gone, why would it be gone?"

"Rah Ven are hunted. We make excellent guards when we are bonded to a location. Some have discovered that this process can be forced upon us. Making us no more than guard dogs," she said.

"At the Watch?" I asked.

"We serve the Watch willingly. One of the few places where we are honored as what we were and are."

"Come, we must not stay out in the open long, even here there are eyes and ears that would betray us," said Luna.

We headed down winding streets and through alleys. She would go down one side street, only to double back and then cut into an alley. In the alley she would find a door, which would take us into a business. We would exit the business after a few minutes and begin the process all over again. After an hour of this she led us to the side of a building that looked like a cathedral.

"In here. We should have lost any spies by now."

"What's in here?" said Meja.

"We are making a small stop to pick up someone you know and then we are heading back to your plane."

We entered the dark of the large building. The vaulted ceilings gave an impression of space. Our steps echoed as we made our way across the floor.

"It's good to see you guys again," said a voice I recognized. It was Zen.

"Zen! Damn, it's good to see you," I said as he gave me a bear hug and forced the air out of my lungs for a moment.

"The Watch?" said Meja.

"Has fallen," said Rin as he stepped out of the shadows. "I must go back, but I wanted to make sure I kept my word to you, warrior. You must go back to your plane. Ascendants are dying and things will only get worse."

"How could a Watch fall? Who could attack a Watch? What about the Rah Ven?" I asked.

"All good questions, warrior. I only know the leader of the attacking force wielded a very large hammer and asked for you by name," said Rin.

At the mention of a large hammer, my blood ran cold. I only knew of one person who used a hammer as a weapon. It was Devin's killer, Roman. Meja visibly blanched when she heard the description.

"Are you certain it was a hammer?" said Meja.

Rin nodded. "I am certain. It had the power to stop, to destroy the Rah Ven." He looked over at Luna who had remained still at his words.

"I am sorry," said Rin.

"There is no need for apologies," said Luna. "If my people fell they did so with honor in service to the Watch."

"Describe this weapon to me," said Meja. Rin gave her the description and Meja's face grew dark.

"You know this weapon?" said Rin.

"Our lives just got much worse," said Meja. "If Aurora is involved, the Harbinger is the least of our problems."

Luna led us to the back of the cathedral where a set of doors held ornate carvings depicting the Rah Ven in both human and canine form. It looked like the scene of a hunt until I looked closer and saw that it was something more... intimate.

"What is this place?" I asked.

"This is a fertility temple. My people are very open about our relations, unlike other species," Luna said as she smiled at me.

"We can use this doorway?" said Meja, changing the subject.

"I must take you through," said Luna. "Only a Rah Ven can keep this portal stable enough for you to use it."

"Fine, the sooner the better. We need to stay on the move, and I need to find my monitor. I don't want to run into Roman as we do this."

"Can he really find us, even here?" said Samir. "It would seem we are quite safe."

"When Aurora was sane and heading the monitors, Roman was her second. He was in charge of bringing in any monitor that went rogue." She paused a moment as if reliving the memory. "It doesn't happen often, but when it does it usually means a loss of life. Rogue monitors are dangerous and deadly."

"Did this Roman stop them?" asked Samir.

"Once Roman was tasked with dealing with the rogues, we didn't lose another monitor. He would find them wherever they hid, even across planes, and use his hammer. No one escaped him once he started looking for you. He was relentless and ruthless. He earned his name."

"What did they call him?" asked Samir.

"They called him the Death Stalker," Meja said as Luna opened the door that led back to my plane.

SIXTEEN

MARA DRESSED KALYSTA'S WOUNDS and made her as comfortable as possible. Sylk had been gone for most of the day and she had begun to worry. She made her way down to the lower level to get something to eat when she heard the voices.

"Fan out, and search the property. He used to come here often thinking he was safe. Make this quick, it won't be long before the Watchers arrive."

It was Rael.

She almost dropped the bowl she held. She crept back upstairs to where Kal lay.

"Kal, Kal," she whispered. Kal came to and opened her eyes.

"Wh—What is it?" she said "Where are we?"

Mara placed a hand over Kal's mouth to silence her.

"Rael is here, we must hide before the Gyrevex find us," said Mara.

She could hear the footsteps outside of the house. In moments they would be inside. She found the panel that accessed the safe room and helped Kal out of bed and into the small room. As the door closed behind them, a Gyrevex entered. It stood still for a moment, taking in the scene, and then left the room. In the safe room Mara let out a breath as the Gyrevex went downstairs.

"We should be good here until they leave," said Mara.

"How did they know about this place? Isn't this some kind of secret house Sylk has?" said Kal.

"I thought as much, but it seems Rael knows more about my master than I do. In any case we should be safe now."

*****

Downstairs, Rael gathered the Gyrevex and began to create a portal.

"Nothing?" asked Rael.

The Gyrevex shook their heads.

"I didn't think he would be here, but fortune favors the thorough."

The Gyrevex stared back at him, silent.

"Try not to speak all at once. I know how to flush out our warrior. We kill two birds with one blade. I think it's time for more ascendants to die, but first we must pay someone a visit." He looked around the house as the portal formed itself before him.

"This is actually a cozy home. Burn it down," he said and then stepped into the portal.

SEVENTEEN

NEW YORK CITY WAS A HIVE OF activity. I loved and hated my city in equal measure. For all its size, I realized that it was small compared to the planes I had visited in the last few days.

"We must be careful, Dante. The Lotus will be waiting for us," said Meja.

The Black Lotus. I hadn't given them much thought since we left for the Records. They were an assassin team sent from the Warriors of the Way. They thought I had gone rogue. After what Meja did to Diana, I didn't think they were too far off base. At first they wanted to bring me in, to control Maelstrom. Now it was kill on sight. Not just me, but anyone who helped me.

"Will they be pissed after Diana?"

Meja gave me a withering glance.

"They won't be pleased. She will be replaced by her second, Monique. They will keep the triad intact."

"Great, because we don't have enough to worry about," I said.

"Actually, we can't pay attention to that right now. Hopefully we can remain under their radar, but we have to focus on the Harbinger and avoid Roman at all costs," said Meja.

We blended into the crowds in midtown Manhattan, just another group of New Yorkers going somewhere in a hurry.

"Why him? It would seem Roman is as much a threat as Rael," I said.

"Roman probably wants you alive for some purpose Aurora has planned. Rael, on the other hand, just wants the weapon. That does not require you to be alive for very long. In fact he probably prefers you dead."

"That's comforting," I said.

"Those are the facts. We focus on the greater threat first, and right now that threat is Rael and the Gyrevex," she said.

We turned on 42nd Street and headed to the public library.

"There are some old spaces in there we can use to stay off the Lotus's radar," said Meja. "We need to stop Rael and that means finding the ascendants of this plane."

"How are we going to do that?" I said. I had no clue how we were supposed to find an ascendant. I knew they were important and that I may be one. That didn't mean I knew what one looked like.

"*We* are not going to do anything. Since you have the use of your inner sight, you are going to use that to point us in the right direction," she said.

"Can't you locate them another way?" I didn't look forward to using my inner sight. It always left me feeling out of sorts and disoriented.

We reached the front of the library. The sun blazed down 5th Avenue as we walked around to the side of the building. The doors on the 42nd Street side had been sealed for decades. I recognized the bas relief on the old brass doors and saw the owls in flight. It was the symbol of the monitors. Meja pushed several of the non-descript decorative elements in a particular sequence. The door whispered open and we entered a cool dark room. Diffuse light filtered in from the large windows. We were in some kind of meeting room.

"Your inner sight is the fastest way. Any other method we can use will alert Rael to our position," said Meja. She began to arrange the furniture and seemed to be looking for something in one of the desks.

"This should help. It's a focus," she said as she handed me a small prism. "It should help mitigate the disorientation and keep you under the radar. We don't want Rael knowing where we are."

"Which is bad for us," said Zen.

"Not for us, unless Kriyas are involved," she said as she looked at me. "Then it's bad for us. Sit down here." She motioned me to a chair, and the rest of the group moved off to the side while Zen stood by the door.

"When you use your inner sight, make sure your weapon doesn't manifest. We just want to know how many ascendants are left in the city. If your weapon appears we may as well stand on the tallest building and scream for Rael," she said.

"We just need a count? What's the point of this?" I said.

"All ascendants are connected on some level. This will help us determine how many are left. You won't have to count, you will just know."

"Then what?" I still didn't know why she wanted to know how many ascendants were left. I knew she wasn't telling me something.

"Make sure your weapon stays within, warrior," she said as she stepped to the side.

I didn't have much practice using my inner sight. It allowed me to see the true nature of things and most of the time that was unpleasant. Using it like this was new for me. I sat back in the chair holding the prism and closed my eyes, letting my mind be still. I felt my chi flow around me and pool in the center of my forehead. With my eyes still closed I was able to 'see' in a different spectrum. I kept still and felt for the ascendants. I didn't know what to look for— and then I felt the tug. I felt a tether in my center that connected to something.

"I feel something," I said.

"Follow that feeling. It should be your connection," said Meja.

I mentally traced the feeling. It felt like a latticework of strands going in every direction. I knew how many strands there were as sure as I knew my name.

"Fifty," I said. It was the number that came into my head. I opened my eyes and saw her shake her head.

"Shit, are you sure? There's no time," she said.

"I'm sure. Time for what?"

"Focus again. This time find the closest one to us."

I closed my eyes and repeated the process. "He is close— about ten blocks away, south from here. I don't have an address but I can show exactly where he is," I said.

"How do you know it's a he?" said Zen.

"I just do."

"That's good. Let's get ready to move," said Meja.

"Why are we doing this?"

"Do you know what an ascendant is?"

"I have an idea—"

"They are what stand between us and this plane falling into Lucius's hands. Some of them know they are ascendants, many have no idea. Once the number falls below one hundred ascendants on any given plane, the barrier between planes weakens."

"That explains the Harbinger," said Samir.

"Exactly. If that number falls below twenty ascendants, this plane falls."

"This is a hub plane—if it falls…" started Luna.

"Then every plane connected to it falls," said Meja. "Unless this plane is sealed off."

"We can seal off three planes?" I asked.

"Nine planes. Three connected to this one and two connected to each of those. This is the hub," said Meja.

"That would mean—" began Samir.

"No more portals, no more travelling, no more threat," said Meja

"No, you cannot do this. It would strand the other planes. It would mean no warriors to assist in times of crisis. We do not know if the process is reversible after the last time," said Samir.

"The last time?" I asked.

"At one point it was twelve planes, until the hub closed off the access to one of the triads," said Samir.

"To prevent destruction to all. The plane had been overtaken by disease that we had no cure for," said Meja.

"The disease was never proven and the triad still stands stranded. The hub was never able to reestablish a connection," said Samir. "We do not know what happened to a countless number of beings."

"This is ancient history," said Meja.

"The lesson still stands, monitor. We cannot abandon the other planes."

"It would mean each triad stands alone, without the hub. It has been done in the past," said Meja.

"And resulted in civil war as the planes warred against each other," said Samir. "The hub is the stabilizing force."

"We are down to fifty ascendants. I would say this is a crisis," said Zen.

"We are not going to let that number fall any lower than it is right now. But we can't stop the Harbinger on our own," said Meja.

"We must try. I can teach the warrior the words—"

Meja exploded. "His weapon is tainted! It belongs to an entity we are trying to stop. Don't you understand we don't have another choice?"

"Monitor, there is always a choice," said Samir.

Meja gathered her things and stuffed them in her pack.

"This plan of yours; teach him the words, and then what? He defeats Lucius with his own weapon? Why not just kill him now?" she said as she looked at Dante. "You would be doing him a favor."

"When you say it like that it doesn't sound like such a good plan," said Zen.

"How would you like me to say it? I'm not going to sugarcoat it just so you can feel like heroes on your way to save the plane. The best outcome of this mission is suicide."

"We cannot abandon them, monitor," said Samir as he placed a hand on hers.

"I'm trying to save them, don't you see?"

"You must have faith in your companions, in the warriors around you. We are not so weak. Perhaps we can make the difference."

"Can we put the ascendants in the mirror?" I said. "A place like where Mariko was that would keep their connection to this plane, but keep them out of harm's way and not drive them psycho?"

Everyone looked at Meja and I realized that she was the emotional center of our group.

She paused a moment. "It's possible, but it would be the same as imprisoning them. How is that any better?" said Meja.

"It would buy us time, not much I admit, but maybe enough for us to stop Rael," I said. "We could ask them to help us. The alternative is to be hunted down by Rael."

She nodded. "I know of a place that can serve this purpose, where they would not feel uncomfortable. This is a temporary measure at best. We will have to prevent Rael from killing more ascendants," said Meja.

"Let's go save some ascendants," I said. The words had just left my lips as the large windows shattered, sending glass in every direction. The Black Lotus had found us.

EIGHTEEN

SYLK APPROACHED A RAH VEN. It was one of the few that remained. This one was older and some of its coat was covered in gray hair.

"Peace, old one," said Sylk.

"Peace, Karashihan. I am Grawl," said the Rah Ven.

"You have lost much today. My heart is with you."

The Rah Ven remained in canine form as he padded closer to Sylk. He looked into Sylk's eyes a moment before speaking.

"Your words are true. We are saddened by the loss, but we do not mourn. They died in service to the Watch. It was an honorable death, one befitting one of our kind."

"I cannot bring them back, but I can try and prevent more of this death," said Sylk.

"Make your request. I have many to tend to."

"The Keeper said to look to you for the location of my companions," said Sylk.

"Did you know we are hunted, Karashihan? Like dogs we are pursued. We are enslaved and bonded against our will across the planes. They steal the little ones from their families and slaughter us with no remorse."

Sylk remained silent. He knew of the plight of the Rah Ven.

"You will do something for me, Karashihan. You say you want to prevent more of this"—Grawl looked around at the bodies of the slain Rah Ven lying in the courtyard—"then you will stop those who hunt our young, ripping them from their homes and enslaving them."

"Who is it, old one?" said Sylk.

"You may know of them. They call themselves the Mikai," said Grawl.

Sylk looked into the eyes of the Rah Ven, his jaw set. "What you ask is no small thing, old one. These are the most deadly assassins in all of the planes."

"It is why I ask it of you. That is my condition. Do you accept?"

If Sylk agreed he would be sworn to bring those responsible for hunting the Rah Ven to justice. If they were part of the Mikai, it could mean his life.

"You have my word, old one. I will find those responsible and bring them to justice," said Sylk. "The sword or the scroll?" He was giving the Rah Ven the opportunity to mete out the type of justice to the accused. One was swift and final—death. The other would bring those accused before their accusers.

Grawl fixed his yellow eyes on Sylk. Then he growled.

"A hundred years ago I would have said the scroll. There are far too few of us now because we avoided the sword. Take them the sword, Karashihan," said Grawl.

"As you wish," said Sylk. "My companions?"

"They are with one of my pack mates. She is called Luna. They are in the hub plane."

Sylk looked at the destroyed obelisk, which would have given him a portal to the hub.

"I cannot travel there directly," said Sylk.

The shortest path is through my home," said Grawl. "You cannot travel there alone. You are not Rah Ven."

"Will you accompany me, old one?"

"I cannot. I have been bound to this place for too long. Perhaps this will help you," said Grawl as he shifted to his human form and gave Sylk a pendant that had been hanging around his neck.

The pendant was in the shape of a Rah Ven fang. As a human, Grawl looked like an older man with grizzled features. His wiry frame was covered in hair. He stood a head taller than Sylk. Only the eyes remained unchanged, glowing a deep yellow, the color of honey in sunlight. He was dressed in flowing robes that denoted his position as pack leader among the Rah Ven.

"This should allow you passage. It says you are part of my pack. If you are stopped, present this pendant," said Grawl.

Sylk bowed. "Thank you, old one."

"Call me Grawl. You are part of my pack now. Remember your words, and let your actions match them, Karashihan."

"Run long, run fast, Grawl."

Grawl nodded and shifted back to canine form. He headed back to the Watch, leaving Sylk alone.

"Time and circumstance change us all," said the Keeper as he strode beside him.

"The cost of his help was steep," said Sylk.

The Keeper placed a hand on Sylk's shoulder. His grip was a vice.

"You should leave here now. I am afraid we will have more violence before the day is done," said the Keeper. "Keep your wits about you in their plane. That pendant can bring you trouble if used against you. Before you go to the hub, you are needed elsewhere. My apologies for your rapid departure."

"What do you mean, more violence?" said Sylk as the Keeper shoved him back and out of the plane.

*****

The Keeper had forced Sylk out of the plane with a thought. He had sensed his new visitor.

"I love what you've done with the place. Renovations?"

The Keeper turned to face the speaker.

"Harbinger, as you can see you are too late. The one you seek is not here and I do not know where he is."

"I noticed," said Rael, looking around. "Seems someone was very upset."

"The warrior is not here and I cannot help you," said the Keeper.

Rael drew his swords. The energy arced between them as he held them in front of his body.

"That's where you're wrong. I think you can help me," he said.

The Keeper brought his staff before him, his eyes focused on Rael.

"You and I share a similar trait. I heard you can't die as long as the Watch stands," said Rael. "We both know this is not the true Watch." He swept an arm around the courtyard.

"You must not do this, Harbinger," said the Keeper.

"I know that the real Watch lies beneath our feet." said Rael.

The Keeper remained silent, his face grim.

 "I can't die either," said Rael. As long as my master lives, he will keep me alive, but maybe you are powerful enough to test that theory. What do you say, *sensei*? Can you kill me?" said Rael as he attacked with both swords.

NINETEEN

MARA SMELLED THE SMOKE first. Not daring to open the safe room for fear this was ruse to draw them out, she stayed back. The heat was next followed by panic—Kal's.

"They're trying to burn us!" said Kal. "We need to get out of here. We need to get out. Need to get out."

Kal got up and headed for the door on unsteady feet.

"Can't die in here. Won't die in here, let me out, Mara," said Kal as she tried to get past Mara.

"Wait, Kal. This could be a trick. This is Rael we are dealing with. Take a breath and let me check outside," said Mara in a measured tone. Each word was deliberate and she kept eye contact with Kal as she sat her down on the makeshift bed.

"Let me check if this is a real fire," said Mara. "I promise to come back for you."

Mara slid open the door and was greeted with searing heat. The flames had taken over the lower level and were engulfing the upper level.

Those are real. How the hell do we get out of this?

She reached back in and grabbed Kal.

"We need to leave, now," said Mara.

She took a blanket from the bed and wrapped Kal in it. Dousing it with water they made their way to the window. The wooden slats were weakened by the fire. Mara's hands were surrounded with purple energy as she broke the slats.

"We are going to have to jump from here, Kal," said Mara.

Kal was unresponsive. Her eyes were fixed on the flames.

"I don't want to burn. Don't let me burn. Don't let me burn," Kal whispered as Mara lifted her up and dropped her outside of the house. Mara looked one last time around the room. The flames were licking up the walls and the heat was becoming unbearable. She jumped out of the window landing bedside Kal, who was moving away from the house and the fire.

"Are you hurt?" said Mara.

Kal stood up and started running. Mara kept pace behind her.

"Kal, stay close. It's dangerous out here," said Mara, looking around.

"I'm not going near that," said Kal as she slowed.

This is bad. We need to get out of here. We need Sylk, before the Watchers arrive and erase us, thought Mara. *Master, where are you?*

"You're right, we need to keep moving. We can't stay here. Let's go, but stay close to me," said Mara.

It seemed Kal had returned to her senses as they headed into the forest that surrounded the still-burning house.

"What happened to you?" said Mara.

"I don't want to…I can't talk about it—thank you, though. If I had been alone I don't think I would have made it out," said Kal.

"We are all pursued by demons. I understand," said Mara. *If we don't get out of here soon we will be pursued by something much worse.* The image of Anna reduced to nothing flashed in her mind and she picked up her pace.

Behind them a pair of eyes followed their progress. The figure leapt silently from branch to branch, staying close.

TWENTY

GLASS WAS EVERYWHERE AS black- clad bodies rappelled into the space. I was still disoriented from using my inner sight, but I knew this was bad. We were surrounded in seconds. She came in through the door. A tall blonde dressed in a black body suit covered in knives. She held a dagger in each hand and stopped just inside the door, letting her eyes adjust to the change in light.

"You let him use his inner sight ,Meja. Why would you do that? You had to have known we would be waiting for something like that," the woman said as she entered the room.

"Monique, how's Diana?" said Meja.

"You bitch," said Monique as she blurred her hands and threw her daggers.

Meja's sword appeared instantly. She deflected one of the daggers and side-stepped the other.

Two more daggers appeared in Monique's hands.

"I can do this all day," said Meja.

Monique smiled. "I'm sure you can. What about them? Can they do *this* all day?" she said as she began to rapid fire daggers at all of us.

Several of the daggers found targets. I managed to stumble out of the way as my sense of bearing returned. Zen and Luna were not so lucky. Zen caught a dagger in the thigh and Luna had one in her arm when Monique was done.

Meja advanced on Monique, sword in hand.

"Stop where you are or I will kill you all," said Monique. She had her hand raised. All around us the members of the Black Lotus aimed pistol crossbows at us.

"I won't make the same mistake Diana made, Meja," said Monique.

Meja stopped. My head finally cleared as I realized the situation we were in. Samir was standing next to me whispering something I couldn't make out. Inside of me I could feel Maelstrom struggling against my control.

Let me out, vessel. I can take care of this upstart. I only need a few moments, said Maelstrom. The anger rose. We were trying to save not only our plane but every plane connected to ours. How could they not see this? Why would they stand in our way instead of helping us?

Maelstrom appeared in my hands, its black and crimson symbols shining with light.

"Dante, no!" yelled Meja.

Time slowed as I saw the expressions change on those around me. I could hear the others. They were far off voices, a noise hovering below the roar in my ears. Part of me knew this was wrong. I knew this would only make matters worse, but I had lost control and it was too late now. Monique had given the order and the arrows were on their way. Instruments of death coming to claim our lives. Because of me, because of who and what I was. Because I wielded a cursed weapon.

Do what you must, Maelstrom, I thought.

I felt myself recede from my body as it took over, slamming the short staff to the ground. My voice took on that strange dissonance when it spoke through me.

"*Repelare*," I said in that strange voice. A shock wave spread out from the impact of the staff on the floor. The arrows were sent off course. Some of them hit other members of the Black Lotus. Most careened off the walls and bounced harmlessly on the floor. Most but not all. Meja had an arrow buried in her side and Samir had several arrows in his leg. I had been too late and now they were suffering for it.

"You cannot keep them safe, warrior. You failed. Look around, only you remain," said Monique.

I didn't need to look around. I could sense where each of them lay.

"You should have killed me first," I said.

Monique threw several more daggers at me. I swatted them away as I closed the distance.

"Fire at will!" she yelled.

I could hear the fear and panic in her voice and it made me glad. Arrows were flying at me from every direction. I could sense the displacement of air around them and avoided or deflected them. She kept throwing daggers at me, forcing me to move or roll to avoid being hit.

"You have neither the skill nor the expertise to stand before me, child," I said as I slid into melee range.

I jabbed forward with Maelstrom, she parried with her daggers. As I brought the staff back, blades formed on the ends. I swung back. Too late she realized that the blades existed. She blocked the staff as I buried the blade in her leg.

"Ungh," she cried out as I ripped the blade out of her leg sideways doing as much damage as possible. That was when the first arrow hit me. A few seconds later my vision became blurry. More arrows followed the first, burying themselves in my back and legs.

Poison, goddammit. Not fair, I thought. As if fairness had any part in this situation. I collapsed to the ground as hands grabbed me and a second explosion rocked the building.

"Let's go!" yelled Monique. "We have what we came for."

I was picked up as the world tilted around me.

"And the others?" a voice said.

"Let the poison do its work. They are finished," she said.

Once we were outside she grabbed me by the front of my cloak. My eyes focused on her knuckle knives as they glinted in the sun. Rage danced in her eyes. She punched me once, twice and once more. I saw the desire to end me in that moment. It would be a simple thing, a twist of the wrist and she would plunge the blade in my throat instead of hard metal against my head. I felt my face begin to swell. For once I was glad I was poisoned. The pain of the blows came a distant second to the raging pain in the rest of my body as the poison ate away at me.

"Monique," said a voice.

"I'm fine. That was for my leg," she said as she spat on me and limped off. "Bring that trash. We still have much to do."

I felt the now familiar weightlessness of portal travel, and then the world went black.

TWENTY-ONE

SYLK SAW HIS HOME BURNING and knew if Mara and Kal were still inside, they were dead. He looked around the edge of the house and found the blanket used to exit the inferno he used to call a home. He stilled his mind and reached out. The house was empty and he breathed a sigh of relief. He walked back to where the blanket lay upon the grass.

Where did you go, Mara? Who did this? he thought. He knew it was only a matter of time before the Watchers arrived to investigate and erase this place. They were ruthless in their efficiency. Anything that was not native to the plane was removed from existence. He reached out again as he stilled his mind, this time farther into the forest and felt her presence.

Found you, but where are you going? There is nothing but forest here and the beings that live in the forest will not welcome this intrusion.

He headed off after Mara, aware that he was being watched and followed.

*****

Mara found a clearing and stopped to orient herself.

"What are you doing?" said Kal. "You said there were Watchers here. We have to keep moving."

"We need to know where we are going. All I see is forest. It's too damn easy to get lost in here and not even know it," said Mara.

"Do you have a map? Do you know this place? Have you been here before? Does anything seem remotely familiar?"

"No, I don't have a map and this is my first time here." *She's right, this is futile. Without a map we have no idea where we are going,* thought Mara. *Master, where are you?*

"Then we only have one choice. Put as much distance between us and that house. My guess is that the Watchers will go there first," said Kal.

"You're right, let's keep moving, "said Mara.

They headed off at a run. The figure followed, keeping the same distance as before.

"Wait, I think I hear something," said Mara as she stopped again.

"Yeah, it's called a forest."

"Quiet, let me listen," said Mara. The forest had grown still. All Mara could hear was her rapid breathing.

"I don't hear anything," said Kal.

"That's just it. There should be some kind of--"

In the distance she heard a faint roar.

"What the hell was that?" said Kal as she turned around, startled.

"That is the sound of trees being torn down."

From the distance a voice boomed across the forest.

"YOU DO NOT BELONG," said the voice as a tremor raced across the ground and leaves feel off the trees.

"Oh, shit. Is that—" said Kal.

"Watchers," said Mara as the blood drained from her face and ice entered her veins.

*****

Sylk heard the voice and began tracing symbols in the air as he moved. He needed to find Mara before it was too late. The Watchers would start at the house and move outward. He had some time. He ran in the direction he felt Mara was. Once at the house the Watchers would attune to their chi signatures. He would need to mask them before that happened. He kept tracing the symbols as he ran. In the distance he thought he saw them. As he made his way around some trees they disappeared again. He felt her close now but could not see them.

"Mara!" he yelled. There was no point in being subtle since in moments the Watchers would be in pursuit.

"Master?" He heard her response not far from his location. He ran toward her. Trees were all he saw.

"Mara, where are you?" he said.

"I'm right here," she said. Her voice sounded right next to him.

Then he realized what was happening. He was in the midst of an audible tunnel. The forest dwellers, the Onoi, used them to communicate over long distances.

"Are there any landmarks near you? Something distinct," he said.

"It's all trees, Master, in every direction," she said.

His brain raced. They were running out of time. By now the Watchers would have left the house and would be on their trail. The sun was setting and he could see the smoke from the house in the distance. *At least nightfall will offer them some measure of cover,* he thought.

"Mara, listen carefully. The Watchers will be coming soon. I can mask us but we need to be together or it won't work for you or Kal. You need to summon eight of your duplicates and have them run in every direction and then back to you," said Sylk.

"I don't think I have ever controlled more than three, Master."

"You have to try. It is the only way I can find you in time."

"Yes, Master," she said as she materialized eight copies of herself. She trembled as sweat covered her face. The copies were semi-transparent.

"I have them," she said.

"Good, now send them out."

The eight Maras ran off in every direction, each with glowing hands as the forest plunged into darkness. Mara fell to her knees, her hands gripping the ground as she struggled to maintain the copies intact.

Sylk saw a figure running toward him. It looked like a phantom of Mara.

"Have them run back now. Mara?"

The phantom copy grew fainter with each second.

"She is nodding her head," said Kal. "I don't think she can speak right now."

The phantom began heading back and Sylk followed. As he followed, it began to fade into the night. He kept running straight and hoped they weren't too far away. He had no way to gauge how long Mara could hold a copy, much less eight travelling in different directions. He reached the clearing and saw Mara unconscious on the ground. He saw Kal standing a few feet away.

"How did we hear you? I thought you were right over—" said Kal.

"Sit next to her, now!" yelled Sylk.

Kal jumped at the sound of his voice and sat next to Mara. He traced symbols and his hands left trails of gold and silver. As he finished the last symbol he placed his hand on the ground. A twenty- foot circle of symbols erupted to life around them. Each of the symbols pulsed with energy and flowed with color going from red to blue to green to white.

"Can't you just, you know, 'poof', make a portal?" said Kal.

Sylk sat down and then lay on his back, breathing heavy.

"Portal would attract them," he said in between breaths.

"So what, once we're through the portal, we're history."

"These are Watchers. They travel all of the planes. A portal would only slow them down. The best way to fight them is not to," said Sylk.

"Is that what this circle is? Not fighting?"

At that moment the trees around the clearing were flattened as a Watcher approached. This one was different from the one they had faced in the mirror. Standing nearly ten feet tall and wearing a long gray cloak, it strode into the clearing knocking down trees. It stopped several feet away from them.

"Do not make a noise," whispered Sylk.

It pushed back its hood revealing its face. It was an angelic beauty, androgynous in its features with a hint of angularity in the jaw. The skin was a flawless porcelain white framed by the deepest golden hair. Its eyes were two pools of white that made it seem blind.

"YOU DO NOT BELONG," it said as the force of its words uprooted trees across the clearing. It pointed a finger past the trio, into the trees.

"*DISIPAR*," it said. A figure dressed in forest greens fell from the trees and landed in the clearing, convulsing. The Watcher opened its hand and the figure froze.

"YOU MUST BE PURGED," it said as it closed its hand. The figure on the ground disintegrated in a cloud of dust, leaving only the clothing behind. After a few moments the clothing disappeared.

The Watcher stood still a moment and then floated away into the forest.

Sylk let out a long breath as the Watcher faded from sight.

"Who the hell was that, in the trees?" said Kal.

"If I had to guess, I would say Mikai," said Sylk

"Mikai. As in the worst nightmare you can have, Mikai?" asked Kal. "That Mikai?"

"Is there another kind?" said Sylk. "The real question is what were they doing here following you?"

"It's not like we can ask him," said Kal as she looked at the place the Mikai had landed and then been erased.

"Not any longer, no. I know somewhere we can ask," said Sylk as he placed a hand on Mara's forehead. She was still unconscious.

"Where?"

"Get comfortable, we will spend the night here. Tomorrow we ask the Rah Ven," said Sylk.

TWENTY-TWO

THE KEEPER STEPPED BACK AND dodged the double-bladed attack. He swung his staff in a circle as he retreated. Rael brought up both swords to block the staff and was sent back several feet from the impact.

"Excellent," said Rael. "You are more than I hoped for."

"Stop this madness, Harbinger," said the Keeper.

Rael laughed as he attacked again.

"Madness is all I know. Kill me or die."

Rael lunged with one sword and then the other. The Keeper blocked one sword and allowed the other to lunge past him. An electrical discharge left the sword. The Keeper swung the staff in front of him to let it act as a makeshift lightning rod. The bolt hit the staff and arced away.

"You don't have to live like this," said the Keeper.

"I stopped 'living' long ago, Keeper," said Rael as he slashed with a sword, forcing the Keeper to shift right then left. "It's just survival now."

"There is still hope for you," said the Keeper as he pushed Rael back with a wave of energy from his staff. Rael crossed his swords to deflect the blast as he redirected the energy. The wave hit one of the remaining walls of the Watch, punching a large hole in it.

"Hope," said Rael with disgust. "Hope for what? Everything and everyone I cared for was ripped away from me. The only thing I can hope for now is death, and even that is denied me."

Rael turned and wrapped both swords around him as dark energy enveloped his body. The Keeper advanced and struck with his staff. Rael let him. The staff became trapped against his body. Energy raced down the staff and surrounded the Keeper. Still the Keeper did not let go.

"You have a choice, Rael," said the Keeper as the energy from the swords consumed him.

"No," said Rael as the Keeper disappeared.

"I made my choice long ago. There's no going back now."

The Gyrevex drew close to Rael as he sheathed his swords. His body still vibrated with the essence of the Keeper.

"The weapon bearer is in the hub plane. Let's go erase some ascendants— that should draw him out," said Rael.

TWENTY-THREE

WHEN I REGAINED CONSCIOUSNESS I found myself in an empty room. A pair of thick metal bands were around my wrists. Each black band was inscribed with several silver symbols designed to prevent access to my chi. I had seen something like this before. Suppressors. My body felt like one large bruise. Everything ached. I managed to get to a seated position and waited for the room to right itself as I shifted next to a wall.

I tried to reach my center and access my chi. The symbols on the bands flared and the pain was excruciating. Every nerve in my body was on fire. I screamed until my throat was raw, and then I screamed some more. The tears flowed freely as I sought relief and found none. At some point I know I lost consciousness because the pain subsided.

As I opened my eyes again everything was dark except for a rectangle of light I guessed was the doorway. Several figures stood in the middle of the room. I couldn't make out details through the haze of pain that racked my body, but I could breathe. I lay on the floor in a fetal position not daring to move for fear of setting off the pain again.

"I wouldn't try that again," said a female voice. The voice was familiar but the pain was making recollection difficult. Without visual cues I couldn't place it. A boot moved me to a sitting position, setting off new flares of pain in my body. Then it all came back to me—Monique and the Black Lotus. A figure limped toward me using a cane as I shielded my eyes from the light.

"The others," I said, my voice a rasp.

"By now the poison that is merely burning through your body has killed them."

She had a bandage around her leg where I had stabbed her and was dressed in the robes of a monitor. Underneath the robes I could see the glint of the knives attached to her thighs. She crouched down to where I sat, using the cane for support. I saw her wince in pain at the motion. Waving a hand in front my face, she stopped when I reacted.

"Blindness is usually a side effect of the toxin," she said.

"Water," I said.

She laughed then.

"You think you are a guest here?" she said as she waved an arm around and grew serious.

"Water, please."

"Did you know Diana was my teacher? Do you know what a soul siphon does? My teacher, my friend, is a statue for next hundred years or so. She can hear and see but cannot react. She is a prisoner trapped inside her body," she said and anger laced her words.

"Please."

She signaled to one of the figures next to her and a small cup was placed in my hands. My hands trembled as I brought the cool liquid to my cracked lips. It burned on the way down and I spit some of it up: manar.

"I wouldn't waste it. That will keep you alive," she said.

I tried drinking it again. My throat was sandpaper.

"Our initial orders were to kill you on sight," she said.

I coughed and choked on the manar. The pain flared up again bringing fresh tears. She stood up and looked down at me.

"Why…why didn't you?" I rasped.

"If it were up to me, I would end you right now, but it's not up to me," she said. I could see the hatred and contempt in her eyes.

"How long…how long will you keep me here?" I said. I knew this was a cell of some kind.

"You are more useful alive. If we killed you, the weapon you hold would pass to another warrior. We don't want that. I hear warriors live a long time. You are going to be here for the rest of your pathetic life, however long that is," she said.

"My friends…"

"Won't find you. No one knows where you are. Those suppressors were made for you. The pain will never completely fade. If you try to access your chi, well, I can only hope that you try," she said with a smile that never reached her eyes.

"You don't understand. The ascendants are in danger. The Harbinger—"

"Is a myth. There are no ascendants and no Harbinger. How do you think we found you? Who suggested you use your inner sight? Didn't it seem strange to you? You trusted them and they used you."

"You're wrong," I said. "I felt them, the ascendants."

"What you felt were people with latent energy. There are no ascendants protecting our plane. We do that— the Warriors of the Way. Warriors, guardians, the monitors and the Lotus. You have been told a fairy tale and you believed it."

"No, can't be true."

"Ask yourself, would we really leave the safety of our entire plane to individuals who may not even know they are tasked with doing so?"

I remained silent.

"You were lied to. Those who helped you were judged, convicted and treated as we do all rogues. They were trying to take over this plane and were using you to further their plans."

"No." My thoughts were racing. *Could she be right? Could Meja and the rest be rogues using me?*

"I'll leave you to get comfortable. One last thing, *warrior,* we depend on our connection to the other planes for survival. It is only through those connections that we have been able to keep our enemies at bay and peace in the planes. These traitors have been trying to cut us off for decades now. It has been their driving mission. Once we are cut off they can strike without fear."

"No," I said, looking away. My mind was reeling.

"Yes, at some point I'm sure they suggested closing off the plane. Didn't they? Maybe even Meja herself?" she said as she grabbed my chin and forced me to look at her. "Did you care for her? Entertain thoughts about her? How could you be so naïve? She doesn't care about you. You are just a tool to be used. A means to an end."

She limped out of the room with the two figures trailing her. I heard the door slam shut cutting off all sound from outside, but I couldn't silence her words.

*****

Monique walked out of the cell. The pain in her leg reminded her with each step of how close they came to losing this fight. She stepped over to the waiting men, members of the Black Lotus.

"Do you think he believed you?" said Rory, the second member of the triad leadership of the Black Lotus.

"He doesn't need to believe me, he just needs to doubt them," she said.

"He's right about the ascendants, they are in danger—"

"And they will be relocated somewhere safe by *us*. No more interference. No more talk of a Harbinger. We handle this my way. Do you really think the first Karashihan is lurking somewhere ready to come back? How old is he, around five hundred? Spare me the nonsense."

"Well, there are stories," said Rory.

"And that's exactly what they are, stories. Here are the facts. That warrior has an artifact that can undo us all. We keep him suppressed and out of commission. We took down a major threat but that was just a battle in this war. There are other rogues that need to be put down. I'm just glad we finally got that bitch Meja. Sylk is still out there somewhere."

"We were lucky," said Rory.

"When I bury all who have fallen, I'll remember how lucky we were," she said as she walked away.

TWENTY-FOUR

MEJA PULLED THE ARROW OUT of her side. She could feel the poison burning through her. She needed to act fast. In moments her vision and reflexes would be compromised. The Black Lotus used a specific toxin with nasty side effects. One of them was chi suppression. If she didn't stop the effects of the poison soon, it would be too late. She wouldn't be able to access her chi to cause a stasis, stopping the poison. Tracing symbols with her hand, she began. The first time, she missed the sequence.

"Shit," she said and began the sequence again. The edges of her vision were going dark, tunneling in.

The second time she forgot a symbol causing the trail of colors to fade midsequence. *Goddammit Meja, focus. You can do this. You must do this*, she thought. She did the sequence again, forcing herself to go slowly. *Slow is smooth and smooth is fast,* she thought to herself as her throat started to constrict, making it hard to breathe. She was glad she had paid attention in her symbology class. It was why she was a senior monitor. She never understood why it would be important to put her body in stasis, until now. The third time worked and she felt herself being able to breathe as the effects of the poison were lessened.

Holding her side, she went over to where the others lay and repeated the sequence for each. *This will buy us some time, but not much,* she thought as she cleaned and bandaged her wound.

"Monitor, how bad is it?" said Samir.

She treated his wounds, pulling out the arrows and doing her best to clean out the poison. The Lotus always used poisoned weapons. No one knew the antidote, and she wasn't sure there was one. It was what made them so fearsome.

"It's bad. I stopped the poison for now, but it's not an antidote. I don't know if there is one," she said. "I can't open a portal, much less manifest my weapon. The poison is too far along for that."

She felt for the short sword she carried on her thigh. Monitors were trained not to rely solely on chi weapons. Its presence calmed her somewhat. *At least I'm not totally defenseless,* she thought as she adjusted the thigh straps holding it in place.

"How are the others?" asked Samir.

Samir appeared to be doing better than the others even though he was covered in sweat and his speech was slurred. He moved to a seated position on the floor.

"Luna is in the worse shape. It could be because she's Rah Ven and her body is reacting differently to the poison, I don't know. Zen seems to be doing better. Maybe Monique uses less poison on her daggers."

"How long do we have?" he said.

"Does it matter? I don't know the antidote!" she said. *How could I have been so stupid? Of course they would be waiting for him to use his inner sight. It's what I would have done. I underestimated them. That won't happen again.*

"I understand our situation is dire, monitor."

"I'm sorry. I just can't believe I didn't anticipate that ambush. Now Dante is gone. They have him god knows where and the ascendants and Rael..." said Meja.

"Let us deal with the immediate, monitor," said Samir.

"You're right, we need to stop this poison or none of that will matter. We have about two days with our bodies in stasis then things start to break down," she said.

"The effects will get worse?" said Samir.

Meja nodded. "Yes, stasis only slows the poison. It doesn't stop it. In two days stasis won't be effective and the poison will run its course."

"Perhaps the Karashihan can assist?" said Samir.

"Well, if you can bring him here with a cure before the authorities show up to investigate the damage, that would be great. Help me move the others to the next room."

They stood up slowly and pulled the bodies of Luna and Zen to an adjacent area away from the meeting room.

"I will try and find the Karashihan. If he is on this plane I can find him," said Samir sitting in a meditation pose. He slowed his breathing and closed his eyes.

"You are full of surprises for a syllabist," said Meja. *How can he even access his chi? The poison seems to be affecting each of us in different ways.*

"The cover does not always tell the story of the book, monitor. I was not always a syllabist, even though it is my primary calling. Please give me a moment."

Meja remained silent while he continued his breathing exercises. *You and I may have unfinished business, but I really hope you know how to reverse this,* she thought as Samir searched for Sylk.

*****

Sylk had remained awake all night. It was the only way to maintain this type of circle. He thought he had heard the Watchers several times in the night. The image of the Mikai being undone was enough for him to stay awake for several nights.

"Master," said Mara as she opened her eyes slowly. He had her head cradled in his lap.

"You did well. You saved us from the Watchers," he whispered. Most of his focus remained on maintaining the circle.

"Thank you, Master," she said.

"We need to go," he said.

"Didn't you say they could follow us across planes?" said Kal who had woken up.

"Yes, but Mara will leave a chi projection behind. It should serve as a distraction long enough for us leave unseen," he said as he looked at Mara. "How do you feel? Are you up to the task?"

"One projection?"

"Yes, but with enough chi to last after we are gone."

She nodded. "I think I can do that."

"In case we are followed I would rather be someplace I know than having them chase us in unfamiliar territory. We are going to the hub."

"We aren't going to the Rah Ven? What about the Mikai?" said Kal.

"Mikai? How are they involved?" said Mara.

"I don't know yet. Let's get to the hub first, then we can travel there and ask," he said.

Sylk began to execute a different set of symbols. It was a difficult process requiring various levels of focus.

"Can he do this? Keep the circle and open a portal?" Kal asked Mara.

"It is difficult. He once told me it is like trying to play the piano, read a book and count backwards all at the same time."

"That doesn't sound difficult, it sounds impossible."

"He has had a long time to practice," said Mara as she sat down opposite him and began to focus her chi. A projection appeared beside her, seated in the same position.

"Mara," said Sylk. His voice was strained.

"Yes, Master."

"I will undo the circle. The Watchers, once activated, remain vigilant for several days. They will appear once the circle is gone. You send your projection into the forest as soon as the circle is gone. I will open the portal in the next moment and we will leave this plane. Do you understand the sequence of events?"

"Yes, Master."

Sylk undid the circle. In the distance they could hear a roar of destruction.

"Send the projection now. Make sure it will remain after we leave," he said.

The projection of Mara ran into the forest, heading toward the sound. The next moment a portal opened.

"Inside now," Sylk said as he saw the image of a Watcher begin to materialize.

They entered the portal as the Watchers followed the projection of Mara.

TWENTY-FIVE

"I HAVE FOUND HIM. It appears he has just entered this plane," said Samir.

"Can you get a message to him somehow?" said Meja.

"I can try, but this poison. It is interfering with my ability to focus."

"I know, but try, Samir."

"I will do my best, monitor."

She could only hope it was enough.

"He is close now. Beneath us? How can that be?" said Samir.

"The subway. He must be in the subway. There is an old entrance to the subway not far from here. We can access it from here."

"I have attempted to place an image of our surroundings in his mind. I do not know if I was successful. I need to rest," said Samir, his voice tired.

"It's the poison. I'm going to try the subway entrance and see if I can see him. Wait here," said Meja.

Samir nodded as he rested against a wall. Meja rested a hand on her sword as she made her way into the library proper. She headed down the south passage and found the old subway entrance that led directly into the building. Without access to her chi she couldn't operate the mechanism that would open the door. She looked around, making sure she was alone and removed her sword and wedged it in the space between the door and the frame. She managed to open it. *Good thing this is an old door.* The passageway led to the old unused portion of Grand Central-Public Library station that had been closed decades earlier. She saw several figures on the platform. *That can't be right. This platform hasn't been used in years, not even by us,* she thought. The next moment the figures were gone. *The poison. It's getting worse.*

"Meja!" She heard a voice but couldn't see anyone. The platform had gone pitch black.

She held her hands out before her, feeling around. She didn't want to fall off the platform. Without her chi she couldn't sense her surroundings.

"Kal?" she said.

"And Sylk and Mara. We found you!" said Kal as she hugged Meja.

"What's wrong, monitor?" said Sylk.

Meja turned to face the voice. "Dante's been taken by the Lotus."

"What's the matter with your eyes?" said Kal.

"We've been poisoned, and it seems I'm blind," said Meja.

TWENTY-SIX

I DON'T KNOW HOW MUCH TIME passed before the door opened again. I was in total darkness. My only companion was the constant thrum of pain that accompanied every movement. I tried to access my chi in degrees and found that

114

below a certain threshold I could access some of it. It was enough for me to 'see' in the dark. It didn't mean much since the room was empty.

I tried to reach out with my sight to see if I could get an idea of where I was being held. At first I didn't feel any pain and then it was upon me. It felt like a hot poker shoved into the base of my neck and pulled out through the top of my skull. I doubled over in agony, dry heaving as nausea took over my body.

Nothing came up since I hadn't been fed anything except manar. I wasn't hungry, but I could tell I wasn't being nourished. Manar gave you a false sense of fullness. I was slowly starving to death.

The door opened. The rectangle of light filled the room.

Unless her leg had healed since our last talk, I knew it wasn't Monique. Judging from the build this was a male. The figure had a small cup in his hand— more manar. He placed the cup on the floor beside me. I stood up to get a better view of who was serving me. The pain threatened to knock me down again.

"Hello, warrior. Here is your meal," said the figure. *That voice. I know that voice.*

I used what little chi I could to try and get an impression of him. He punched me in the stomach, sending me to the floor.

"I wouldn't do that if I were you," he said.

115

The haze of pain fell on me as I looked up from the floor.

"You will rot in here," he said. He drew close to me and pretended to be sitting me up so I could drink the manar. They made sure I drank every cup. If I spit it up they would bring more and convince me to drink it usually with repeated blows. I learned to drink the first cup.

I tried to focus on his face but he kept his hood down.

"You must try to get past the defenses of the bands. Only you can remove them," he whispered. "That is your only hope of getting out of here."

He straightened me up and handed me the cup. I sipped the liquid while trying to get a look at his face, but he kept his back to me.

"Who…who are—" I started.

He backhanded me across the face. "You will not address me unless ordered to do so," he said. I could feel the blood running down my nose, but I was in too much pain to care. He handed me a napkin for the blood.

I spilled some of the manar, so he took the cup and left the room, coming back a few moments later with another cup.

"Drink it," he said.

I drank it with trembling hands. As he drew close to get the cup he brought his face to my ear.

"I told you I would see you soon. Now find a way to get out of the bands, I left you a tool. I won't be able to get back here again without drawing suspicion. It's up to you now," he whispered.

I slumped over on my side, trying to keep the manar down. He pulled back his hood slightly and I saw his face, but I didn't trust my eyes. He left the room and I still had the napkin. They never left anything with me. Inside the napkin there was something solid. I stayed slumped over and held the napkin to my chest. I don't know how they could see me in total darkness but I had a feeling they could. I felt around the napkin and a small stone fell into my palm. As I felt around it I could tell it was a prism.

I couldn't believe it. I saw him take several blows of Roman's hammer. I saw him die, but in my hands I held a prism. A tool that would allow me to focus my chi.

I had just been served by Devin.

TWENTY-SEVEN

"TAKE US TO THE OTHERS, monitor," said Sylk.

"Do you know of an antidote for Lotus poison?" said Meja as she led them back to the entrance. "I came through here. We are two passages

117

down and one to the left. The room is sealed from the inside. Samir can open it, I hope."

"I didn't know an antidote existed," said Sylk.

Meja accepted this news in silence. She knew it had been a slim chance. No one had ever recorded an antidote to the poison. They arrived at the door and Samir opened it after a few tries. He had grown weaker since Meja had left.

"Welcome, Karashihan," said Samir. "I fear we are in most unfortunate circumstances."

"How did you find me? I saw this room in my mind although I have never been here before," said Sylk.

"It was him," Meja said as she pointed in Samir's direction. "He used one of his abilities."

"It was my limited ability. The poison is doing much damage."

"You managed to put them in stasis? How long?" said Sylk.

"I thought we had two days, but I went blind on the platform so it would seem to be much less than that."

"It could be just the way the toxin is affecting you. Samir can still see," said Sylk.

"So there is no antidote to this Lotus poison?" said Samir.

"None that I know of. It's what makes the Black Lotus so feared by their enemies. The effects vary but it always starts with chi suppression, then loss of motor skills, blindness and usually asphyxiation."

"Master, the guardian is not doing well," said Mara. She had gone to each member, assessing how far the poison had advanced. Sylk went over to where Zen lay. He was cold to the touch.

"The guardian doesn't have much longer. It looks like he may be in the final stage," said Sylk.

Luna stirred behind them and mumbled something. Kal went over to her.

"What is it?" Kal said as she propped her up.

"We have an antidote. The Rah Ven have encountered this toxin before and we have defeated it," said Luna.

"Where is the antidote? Can we make it here?" said Meja, her hopes rising.

"In order to make it we must go to my plane," said Luna. "There is a blood healer there that can do this. We will need what we call a blood change. Blood from a healthy Rah Ven will need to enter your system."

"A transfusion? This will work? Will it reverse the effects?" said Meja.

"I don't know," said Luna.

"We do not have much of an alternative," said Sylk. "We do not have the luxury of time. Luna, I need to put us as close to this healer as possible. I need you to fix this place in your mind and give Samir your hand. Can you do what you did before, Samir?" asked Sylk.

"I will try," said Samir as he took Luna's hand and closed his eyes.

"Do you have it?" asked Sylk.

"It is a faint impression, but I think it can be enough to take us there, "said Samir as he projected the image to Sylk.

"That should be enough," Sylk said as he opened a portal to the Rah Ven plane around them.

TWENTY-EIGHT

RAEL STOOD OUTSIDE THE DOJO. He found that most ascendants practiced a form of martial arts. It was usually the older styles, the more traditional and obscure arts that were out of favor with the modern students, that attracted the ascendant. It also helped that he could sense an ascendant once he got close enough. He sniffed the air as the Gyrevex stood around him. It was late and the last class would be ending soon. It was almost always the sensei or head instructor. He noticed there was no sign outside of the school.

"Perfect. Let's go take a class," he said to a Gyrevex. "You two stay here and make sure we are not interrupted."

He headed up the stairs to the dojo where he could hear the sounds of solitary practice.

"I'm pretty certain that when you woke up this morning you did not imagine that this is how your day, and life, would end," said Rael as he stepped on to the dojo floor.

The sensei, his uniform covered in sweat, turned to face Rael and assumed a fighting stance. He was a short, muscular man with strong features. His dark eyes glistened at this challenge. There was some grey around the temples framing his black hair. His knuckles were gnarled from years of conditioning. He extended a hand to the side and a long staff, a *bo* flew off the rack against the wall and into his hand with a resounding thump. The sensei tapped the bo once on the floor and raised it in a defensive stance.

"I like that, no denial, no excuses, just right down to business," said Rael.

"Harbinger," said the sensei. "You are not welcome here."

Rael drew his swords and assumed a fighting stance that held both swords low.

"Oh, I know that. I am not welcome anywhere, sensei, but this isn't about you. I need a certain warrior to come out of hiding. The only way I can do that is if I— what's the term I'm looking for? — *dispatch* ascendants."

"You will never succeed in releasing your master. The Warriors of the Way will not allow it."

"Allow? Allow? Who are you to allow anything? Who appointed you as the lords of the planes? This is the problem with your group. Too self-important. It's time for a change in management," said Rael.

The sensei stepped forward, thrusting with his bo. Rael stepped back, avoiding the attack. Moving to the side, he threw one sword at the sensei while closing the distance. The sword sliced the arm of the sensei as he rotated away from the blade. He brought the staff in a low arc in a strike designed to shatter knees. Rael leapt over the attack. The sensei anticipated this and lashed out with a side thrust kick, connecting with Rael midair. Rael was sent back and landed on his feet, one of his ribs broken.

"Excellent. I am going to enjoy this more than usual," he said. He took a deep breath, focusing his chi and knitted the bone in his side. The pain made him catch his breath. The Gyrevex began to move forward.

"No, this one is mine. Stand by the door," said Rael.

The Gyrevex moved to the entrance and stood there, a silent sentinel awaiting a command.

The sensei took a deep breath and focused his chi. The staff took on an orange glow as he moved it into a defensive position.

"Finally, a challenge," said Rael as he extended his hand to bring his fallen sword back to him. As the sword travelled back to Rael, the sensei launched an attack. Intercepting the sword and sending it flying across the dojo, he lunged at Rael. Rael parried the attacks as the sensei pressed him with a flurry of thrusts and downward strikes. Rael backpedaled as the attacks intensified. The sensei slid back and launched his staff at Rael's head. Rael slipped the strike, letting the staff rest on his shoulder and slid in, stabbing the sensei. The sensei grunted in pain as the sword entered his abdomen. Rael summoned his other sword to his hand. The sensei brought his staff across, striking Rael in the temple. Rael stepped back, stunned, as the second sword entered his hand. He shook his head as he redirected chi into his swords. Energy arced between the blades and they took on a dark blue hue.

His uniform was soaked in blood and still the sensei attacked. He seemed to pay no mind to the wound as he ducked a sword slash and raised his staff to deflect the energy lancing at him from the swords. The force of the bolts made him take several steps back. Rael advanced as the sensei sidestepped a lunge and then a downward slash. The wound hampered his movement and Rael connected with the next attack, a horizontal slash across the chest. The dojo was filled with the smell of burnt metal and charred flesh as the sensei was hit with repeated attacks of arcing energy. The last bolt of energy caused the sensei to drop his staff. Rael stepped in and kicked it away.

"You lasted longer than most," said Rael.

"My death will not bring you victory, Harbinger. In the end you will fail," said the sensei through clenched teeth.

"I saw this great movie once. Immortal warriors were going around removing each other's heads. They were fighting for a prize and only one of them could have it. They kept saying 'in the end there can be only one'. I'm not fighting for a prize—" he stabbed the sensei in the chest—"but in my version of this story everyone dies. In the end there can be none," said Rael as he removed the sword. The sensei fell to his knees, his blood pooling on the floor beneath him.

"The Warriors of the Way will fight you," said the sensei as he fell on his side.

Rael stood over the sensei as his life flowed down the dojo floor. He crouched down and wiped his blades on the sensei's uniform, leaving a trail of blood and gore.

"Their time has passed. I am here to usher in a new rule," said Rael.

"No one will submit to your master."

"There won't be a choice, sensei. It's submit or die."

"They will stop you," said the sensei with his last breath.

"How can you stop something you don't believe exists?" said Rael as he stood and left the dojo. The Gyrevex followed silently behind.

"One less ascendant standing in the way. We remove a few more and I'm certain we will be paid a visit from the Warriors of the Way. Won't they be surprised to find out I'm real?" said Rael.

The Gyrevex remained silent.

"The next ascendant is not too far from here. Let's go pay him a visit," he said as he sheathed his swords.

TWENTY-NINE

I COULDN'T BELIEVE DEVIN was still alive.

Time was an alien concept to me in my cell. I had no way of marking its passage. It could have been days or hours, I didn't know. The only thing that helped me keep track of time were the regular doses of manar. They seemed to know when I would get hungry and then bring my small cup filled with the clear liquid.

I started accessing my chi in small increments. The prism allowed me to circumvent the suppressor bands to a large extent by focusing my chi. The bands seemed to react to the internal buildup of chi use. Once past a certain threshold, they kicked in the same way a circuit breaker trips when there is too much current flowing. The difference being that the bands didn't interrupt the flow of electricity but the flow of chi. They suppressed the flow while engaging all the pain receptors of the body. It was a perfect design if you needed to control someone who could use their chi. Once the bands were on, the flow of chi was cut off and the pain insured there were no further attempts to access it.

The prism allowed me to bypass the design of the bands by acting as a focal point for the flow. As long as I held the prism I could focus my chi through it and not exceed the threshold controlled by the bands.

I started building a tolerance to the pain. I had to escape. As long as I was being held, the ascendants were in danger of being wiped out. I couldn't let Meja cut off the other planes either. Something told me that would have far-reaching repercussions. The negative kind. I needed to get out before it was too late. I didn't know who to trust, but I knew ascendants existed and had to be protected.

I gradually increased the amount of chi I could use until I could get a feel for where I was. It seemed to be a free standing cube, unconnected to anything else. *Where on earth was I?*

With the prism I was able to expand my awareness even further and found nothing. I went over every square inch of my 'cell' and found that no door existed. It was then I realized that the rectangle of light I saw when they brought me the manar was not a door. It was a portal. I was in the mirror.

Monique's comment made sense now. There was no way anyone could find me here. I didn't even know where 'here' was. My only hope of escape was the manar. They needed to open a portal to bring me the manar.

I needed to escape this cube. The problem with my plan was threefold.

First, I didn't know if I was strong enough to stand. A steady diet of manar kept me alive, but didn't strengthen me. The bands prevented too much motion because our bodies use chi as the driving force of life. Too much activity meant pain. I kept having to tighten the drawstring on my pants, which meant I was losing weight.

Second, the haze of pain was still there. I needed to get the bands off before I tried anything.

Lastly, I didn't know where I was 'escaping' to. I could jump in that portal right into Monique's arms for all I knew.

With the prism, I started by siphoning chi back into my body. I needed to get my strength back. Once I knew I was in the mirror I didn't have to worry about being seen. I tied the prism to the inside of my pants and kept it in close contact with my skin at all times. Taking off the bands was going to be difficult and painful. If my circuit breaker theory was right I would need to overload the bands with the use of chi. I could only think of one way to do that.

I would have to manifest Maelstrom.

THIRTY

S YLK OPENED THE PORTAL ACROSS from the home of the healer. Only Zen had to be supported. The rest of the group were able to walk on their own. Luna approached the door of the small home and knocked. A shuffling step came close to the door.

"Who's there?" said an elderly voice.

"Peace, grandmother. We are in need of your services," said Luna.

"Come back later, it's too damn early," said the voice.

"I'm afraid we will not be able to come later."

The door opened a crack and an elderly woman peeked out from behind it.

"That you, Luna?" said the old woman.

"Yes, grandmother, it's me."

"Well why didn't you say so? Come in, come in. Who are your friends, Luna?" The old woman sniffed the air and then grew still. "These are not Rah Ven."

They stood in her kitchen, which was full of jars of every sort. Vials sat on shelves and the table. It seemed every available empty space had some kind of container on it. They sat Zen down in one of the chairs. His head lolled to one side. Samir took a chair next to him to keep him propped up.

"No we are not, but we need your help," said Sylk. The old woman noticed the pendant around his neck. She drew close to Sylk and reached up. Her yellow eyes glistened as she spoke to him.

"How did you get this?" she said as she held the pendant in her hand. "This is Grawl's mark."

"He gave it to me," said Sylk.

"Did he now? Or did you take it from his cold, lifeless body? Do you know about this, Luna?"

"I do not, grandmother," said Luna looking at Sylk, urging him to explain.

"Grawl told me to show this pendant to all who would question me in my search for those who hunt the Rah Ven," said Sylk.

"They take the little ones, you know," the old woman said, mostly to herself as she let go of the pendant. She fussed around the kitchen, moving jars and vials as she spoke.

"You will do this thing?" said the healer. "You will find them? Stop them?"

"I gave Grawl my word," said Sylk.

"You word, bah! What is your word to me? Why do you bring these two-leggers into my home, Luna?

They reek of arrogance." She turned to face Sylk, craning her neck at him as she spoke. "Your word is nothing to me. I am not Grawl, I need more than your word," the healer said.

"Grandmother..." began Luna. The old woman pointed a finger and silenced her.

"Quiet, pup. He may look young, but this one is old like me. I can smell the years on him. We will do this the old way," she said as she pulled a large knife from one of the drawers.

Sylk stood still, not knowing if this was an attack or some strange ritual. She stepped close to Sylk and pulled the knife across her left palm, cutting a deep gash. She handed the knife, handle first, to Sylk. He grabbed the knife and repeated her action, cutting a deep gash in his left hand. The knife was so sharp he didn't feel the cut for several seconds. When the blood began to flow, the old woman grabbed his hand with hers, mingling the blood. Her grip was a clasp of steel.

"Now you tell me what you will do for the Rah Ven," she said.

"I will hunt those responsible for taking your young and I will bring a reckoning for their actions," said Sylk.

As Sylk spoke the joined hands began to glow red. A fine red mist formed around their hands, and Sylk could see it was their blood infused with chi.

"Your word is your bond, our blood is one now. You are one with the Rah Ven. Our sorrow is your sorrow, our joy your joy," she said.

When she finished speaking, the glow flared for a few seconds, sending warmth through Sylk's hand. The mist dissipated and she let go. Sylk looked at his hand and found the wound had healed, leaving a red scar that seemed to pulse.

"This is a blood scar," she said showing him her palm. "It weighs more than your word to Grawl. Put that thing away," she said, pointing at the pendant. "It will bring you more trouble than it's worth; don't know what Grawl was thinking. If you are stopped you show them this," she said, and pointed at the scar on his hand, which matched hers. "Every Rah Ven will know you are a friend of the pack and show respect."

Sylk bowed to the old woman. "Thank you. Will you treat my companions?" he said.

"Don't thank me just yet. There is a good chance you won't survive your hunt. You are after the night shadows, after all. They are the ones who steal the young," she said.

"The Mikai," said Sylk.

"You may be old, but not old enough to correct me. We know them as night shadows," she said.

"Yes, grandmother," said Sylk.

The healer turned to Luna. "Now that we have that out of the way, let's take care of you and your friends."

"Yes grandmother, they are afflicted with—"

"I know what they are afflicted with. It's the blind death. What kind of healer would I be if I didn't know?" She turned to Sylk. "You aren't afflicted. I don't smell it in you. You will be my hands."

Sylk nodded as she handed him vials filled with different liquids.

"This is an evil poison, made by you two-leggers. We call it the blind death," said the healer.

She walked into a room adjoining the kitchen that had a large sink and more tables covered with mortars and pestles. She grabbed a powder from one shelf and put some in a bowl. Grabbing two powders from another shelf she put it in the same bowl. Taking one of the vials she poured the contents into the bowl.

"Mix that, careful not to get any on you. You will be no use to me asleep," she said.

Sylk began mixing the ingredients until they were a thick paste. The room next to the one they were in was full of beds. The healer pointed to it.

"Get your friends in those beds. We need to do a blood exchange and they can't be moving about while it's happening," she said.

Sylk nodded as he left to get the others.

"Get the large one first— he's the worse of the lot," the healer yelled after him as he went to the next room.

Sylk came back carrying Zen and placed him in a bed, and in a few moments every member of the group was also lying in one. The healer had jars filled with a viscous red liquid.

"This here is Rah Ven blood, freely given and freely taken," she said, making a guttural sound that was half growled and half spoken. The liquid in the jars took on an incandescent glow.

"What is this process? This blood exchange?" asked Sylk.

"For the warrior there is blood in life and life in blood. With the blind death the blood is tainted and must be replaced or strengthened to fight the poison. That's what these beds are for and this is why you need a blood healer."

She placed one jar in one of the openings at the head of each bed. For Zen she placed two jars of the blood. Over Meja's bed she placed a jar of blood and a clear liquid.

"We will bring back your sight, young one," she said as she patted Meja's arm.

All the beds had channels running alongside the edges. Each jar had a spigot on the bottom. Once the jars were in place she turned the spigots, releasing the blood. The blood flowed into the channels and surrounded the body of each poisoned member of the group. She handed Sylk a brush.

"Put the paste on them. Careful not to get any on yourself. You're too big and heavy for me to have to move," she said. "The rest of you" —she looked at Mara and Kal—"can wait in the other room."

Sylk applied the paste to each of the group, and within seconds they were in a deep sleep. The healer stood at the foot of the first bed, which was Zen's. She put her hands in the blood. Nothing happened for a few moments and Sylk began to wonder if there was any truth to this healing process. In seconds, tendrils of blood shot out from the channels and embedded themselves in Zen's body. She repeated the process with each one and then sat in a chair beside the beds, visibly tired.

"The process has started. No stopping it now until it's run its course. A few hours and your friends will have the poison out of their bodies. There is nothing you can do now. You may as well wait with the others."

Sylk turned to leave the room and she grabbed his arm, stopping him.

"You have much conflict in you. I smell darkness around you, fighting the light. You must get rid of this taint or it will destroy you and those around you." She let go of his arm and turned to watch the flow of blood over the beds.

Sylk remained silent as he left the room to join the others.

It was then that the growls started.

THIRTY-ONE

I FELT STRONGER WITH EACH passing day. I don't know if there were days that passed or not. I counted by manar servings. I expected I would get one cup of manar daily. It was enough to sustain me the entire day but then I would feel hungry come the next day. If I was being given one cup per day, it had been ten days since I had gotten the prism and began redirecting my chi.

I was exercising and I could feel my strength returning. I started pushing on the bands, drawing more and more chi until the pain was too much to bear. Then I would stop and rest. Each day I was able to hold out a little longer. Being on the manar diet didn't help much but I thought I was ready to test the bands. I waited until the manar was given for the day.

I sat in the center of the room and slowed my breath until it was completely under my control. I focused my chi and began to project outward. The pain was intense, but manageable until the prism literally shattered. A wave of pain washed over me. I was in and out of consciousness a few times when I stopped. My breath was ragged and I was drenched in sweat.

I gathered up the pieces of the prism and joined them together. I tried focusing my chi through it but it wouldn't work as a focus. I threw it against the wall in frustration, realizing what a bad idea that was after the fact. Pieces of the prism would be all over the floor when the next delivery of manar would arrive.

Compartmentalize the pain. Separate yourself from it. Focus your chi and summon your weapon, Owl's familiar voice said.

Owl? No response. *Now I'm hearing voices. Great.* I had to try it. This was the strongest I was going to get. Without the prism my strength would degenerate to where I was before, slowly wasting away.

I centered myself again and began to focus my chi. The pain rushed up immediately. I took the pain and put it aside. I mentally stacked each wave of pain in a box and put that box somewhere else. The waves were coming harder and faster, rocking my body. The symbols on the bands glowed bright silver.

Vessel, what have you done? Maelstrom.

I never thought I would be glad to hear that voice in my head.

I have suppressors on and they inhibit my ability to access you. Even now. I need you to manifest fully, I said in my thoughts.

You do not know what you ask. A full manifestation can kill you. And while I may be amenable to that as a solution it would not benefit me in this place. It would mean surrendering your free will.

I could feel my body giving way to the pain. The glowing symbols were so intense I could feel them burning into my skin. My body began to convulse and I could feel my chi slipping away.

Do it. Do it now. I won't have another opportunity. You will be trapped here with me for as long as I live, I said as I felt my chi slip away. *Too late.* The symbols on the bands did not diminish in intensity.

"What the hell?" I said as the bands began to crack.

I smelled cooking flesh and was instantly hungry and horrified at the same time. It was the smell of my arms being branded by the symbols. Along the cracks I could see crimson lines of energy form. I held my arms away from my body and as far away from my face as possible. The lines grew brighter and brighter until the bands shattered, sending shards in every direction. For a second I thought I had lost both my arms below the elbows. I couldn't feel anything. When I looked I saw the symbols from the bands burned into the skin. The next moment I felt myself recede but not completely.

I will take your offer at another time. For now I will assist you in exiting this place, said Maelstrom.

The weapon didn't manifest in my presence, but I could feel the power coursing through me. *Was it the symbols on my arms?* I would have to investigate that later, but for now I needed to prepare. They would be bringing manar and I would be ready.

THIRTY-TWO

THE HEALER'S HOME WAS SURROUNDED by Rah Ven, some in canine form. The growling grew worse by the second.

"Send them out, grandmother," said one of the Rah Ven in front of the mob.

The healer opened her door with force and stared down the mob.

"I will not. You are welcome to come in and try to remove them," she said.

"How could you heal two-legged scum? They are the ones that steal our young and enslave them!" said another from the crowd.

The healer gave the speaker a hard stare. "You dare speak to me with that tone of voice? I wiped your bottom before you were off your mother's teat.

"Who speaks for this group? Or are you just a bunch of stray dogs too afraid to face me and would rather bark from the shadows?" she said.

One of the Rah Ven stepped forward from out of the mob. He was taller than the rest. His muscular body, covered in scars, rippled as he walked. His long brown hair was cut short, the opposite of most Rah Ven that wore their hair long. His yellow eyes shone with malice as he locked stares with the healer.

"I speak for this group, old one," said the muscular Rah Ven.

"Of course you do, Cane, I should have seen your hand in this," said the healer.

Behind the healer, Sylk stepped into view.

"There he is!" yelled someone from the crowd. "Give him to us. We will have justice for our young!" said another.

"He is my guest," said the healer.

"He has no right to be here," said Cane.

Behind the healer, Sylk raised his left hand showing it to the crowd. A murmur raced through the Rah Ven.

"He has a blood scar?" said a voice.

"How can he have a blood scar? It must be a trick," came another voice.

Cane narrowed his eyes at the scar. The healer smiled at him. Then Cane smiled back.

"I invoke the rite of acceptance," said Cane.

The healer frowned. "He is a friend of the pack. The rite holds no merit. His status has been established, by Grawl," she said as she pulled out the pendant holding Grawl's mark.

There was more whispering among the crowd. Cane raised his hand to calm them down.

"Is Grawl here? Can he confirm this? The rite still holds. I invoke it as a member of the pack and as Rah Ven. He must accept it. You know the alternative," said Cane.

The crowd began murmuring as they grew uneasy. Sylk could see the unease on many of their faces. They did not want to challenge a blood scar and the mark of Grawl. However many of the faces were twisted by their hatred. They wanted revenge for the ones they had lost to the Mikai.

"We accept the rite. He needs time to prepare. We will meet in one hour at the appointed place," said the healer and slammed the door.

"Curse Grawl, and curse this pack," she said under her breath.

"Why curse Grawl?" said Sylk.

She drew close to Sylk as she spoke. "Because he left this pack without a successor. Cane has been trying to take control of it ever since he came of age and I fear today he may have found the opportunity he was looking for."

"What is this rite?" Sylk was not as familiar with Rah Ven culture as he would have liked to be in that moment.

"Since you bear a blood scar and wear Grawl's mark, it makes you a candidate for pack leader. The rite determines if the pack will accept your membership into the pack. It also establishes where you fall in its hierarchy."

"Where do I fall now?" said Sylk.

"Right now you are seen as a threat. If the rite is not completed they will attack as a group. And be within their right to do so," she added.

"Does everyone in my group have to pass this rite?"

She looked away. "No, you act for the group. If you succeed they will be safe."

"If I fail?" said Sylk.

He knew where this was headed. He realized that Grawl had maneuvered him into this position—first, by securing his promise to deal with the Mikai and then by giving him the pendant. The old pack leader knew what would be set in motion the moment Sylk set foot in the Rah Ven plane.

"The rite of acceptance is a fight," she said. "Victory can be determined in several ways. It can be first blood, concession, or death. The challenger picks the method."

"If I succeed, the pack will leave us alone?"

141

"Yes, but if you fail your group shares your fate. Cane always picks death."

THIRTY-THREE

THE TIME PASSED AS I SAT and evaluated where my strength was. Maelstrom would not manifest, even though I tried several times to bring it forth. However, I felt stronger than I ever had. The glyphs on my arms were red and angry but healed. I managed to pick up most of the prism parts and hid them in my shirt. My chi flowed and I was able to sense everything around me. It was a lot of nothing.

Focusing my chi, I summoned small orbs to float around me. I practiced sending them off into the walls until I could penetrate the stone.

Getting out of the cell was my priority, but I had a larger problem. Could I return to the group? Who could I trust? Were they just using me as Monique said? I had no way of proving it. Monique had every reason to lie. Her words were suspect at best. I still needed Samir to master the words of power. But why did Meja want me to use my inner sight? How many times did she suggest I was better off dead? It seemed I was better off alone. If Monique was telling the truth, I was alone and the group was dead, except for Sylk, Mara and Kal. At least if I was on my own I wouldn't be vulnerable to anyone manipulating or using me. I wouldn't be hurt again. That would have to wait. First I needed to get out of this cell. If I could find Devin maybe he would have some answers. It seemed like hours had passed before I felt the surge of energy that signaled a portal was opening. I didn't shield my eyes from the glare as that would have shown the bands were missing.

I sat with my back to the portal. The shadow of the figure loomed over and passed me as he drew closer to bring me my manar. I moved to the shadows, shuffling as I usually did when the pain had control of my body. They considered me a minimal threat and never sent more than one monitor at a time. I could understand the reasoning. Before the bands had come off, I was a minimal threat. I could barely stand, much less put up a fight. With the bands off, I would be a real threat. I had created several orbs as I felt the time for manar approach. I kept them in the shadows as the portal emerged.

"Time for your meal," said the figure. He took several steps toward me and then stopped. "Wait a minute, that can't be right—"

Readers— that's how they knew my state. By reading my aura and intentions they knew I was harmless. He must have picked up on the change in my chi level right away. I didn't give him time to react and sent the orbs at him with a thought. I didn't kill him, even though every cell in my body wanted to destroy those who had put me in this place. He was most likely given a shift to attend to the 'prisoner'. It was Monique I wanted.

The cup of manar fell to the floor and shattered. He followed as the orbs pummeled him senseless. I took his robes and put them over my own clothes. The hood cast my face in shadow. As long as I didn't speak to anyone, I should be able to pass for a monitor. Unless I ran into another reader.

"It's not right, it's perfect," I said as I stepped into the portal.

THIRTY-FOUR

"HAVE YOU EVER FACED A Rah Ven in battle before?" said the healer.

Sylk shook his head. "I have never had the occasion to fight Rah Ven. It is not something I would have attempted alone."

"Smart man," said the healer. "We Rah Ven are ferocious fighters. Our ability to camouflage makes it nearly impossible to see us and the ability we have to skip time makes it almost impossible to hit us."

"Are there any rules to this fight?" said Sylk.

"He must not shift to canine form because you are not Rah Ven. No time skipping or camouflage. You cannot use any special ability outside of your wits or natural ability with the weapon of choice. You will decide the weapon," said the healer.

"I am trained in many weapons."

"Pick the one you are most comfortable with," said the healer.

"What if he is skilled with it as well? Shouldn't I pick something that puts him at a disadvantage?"

"It doesn't matter what you pick, he won't follow the rules. As soon as he feels threatened he will shift to canine form. You must defeat him as a canine. Once he shifts you can use whatever you know, but you must beat the Rah Ven," she said.

"What are my chances?" said Sylk.

"Not bad. The blood scar will give you the strength and reflexes you need if you don't fight for too long. The important piece is the pendant. As long as you stay close to him, Grawl's pendant will stop the camouflage and time skip."

"How close?"

"In the circle of claws," she said as she drew close to Sylk. When she was close enough to touch him with an outstretched finger, she stopped.

"This close," she said.

"Close enough to kill," he said.

"Close enough to die.

"None of your group may interfere or you will unleash the mob and we may all be lost." She said these words looking at Mara and Kal.

"I don't like this, Master," said Mara. "Can't you just make a portal so we can leave?"

"We are not leaving them behind," said Kal, her arms crossed and her jaw set.

Mara shot her a dark look and turned back to Sylk, pleading with her eyes.

"We can come back for them, after things calm down," said Mara "Please don't do this."

"Your master cannot leave. He has given his word and his blood. Bonds that cannot be broken," said the healer.

"They are right," said Sylk, looking at Mara. "I must do this or we put everything in jeopardy."

"What if you fall?"

"Then it wouldn't matter anyway. I will do my best not to fall before Cane," said Sylk.

He turned to the healer. "Any last words of wisdom?"

"I'll not be at the ritual. Someone has to watch the flow of blood to your sick ones. No one but me can do it proper. If Cane finds himself on the losing end of things he may send some of his pack mates to visit your friends. It's not beneath him," said the healer as she looked at Kal and Mara. "Your friends and I will be here to greet them good and proper if they come."

"Thank you," said Sylk.

"Don't thank me. I do this because of the blood scar. A lone wolf is a dead wolf. You heed me?" said the healer.

"I understand. I'll be on my own when things get deadly," said Sylk. *It would not be the first time.*

She nodded and pulled him close.

"Dead never saved anyone. When it's kill or be killed make sure you be the one doing the killing. No hesitation—hesitation is weakness to the Rah Ven. Be swift and be certain," she said as she opened the door and led him to the meeting place of the Rah Ven.

THIRTY-FIVE

I DIDN'T RECOGNIZE WHERE I was at first. Everything was dim and it took a moment for my eyes to adjust to the lighting. It looked familiar, the way most dojos will look after you have been in enough of them. Then it hit me. I was in the nexus dojo, where all this began. I was in the home of the warriors, monitors and Black Lotus. Things just went from bad to nightmarish. I pulled the hood a little lower over my face and looked around. It appeared I was in some kind of supply room and kitchen. Surrounded by food, my stomach grumbled.

I grabbed a large piece of bread, and some assorted meats.

"Hungry, huh? Yeah, that poor bastard can't eat any of that," said a voice. "If you ask me it's criminal what they are doing to him. You can't live on manar for long, no matter how powerful it is."

I froze.

Keeping the voice behind me, I nodded. I couldn't let anyone realize I had escaped—not until I was ready. I didn't know my way around this dojo well enough to navigate the miles of passageways alone. I backed up a few steps as I summoned orbs in front of me. They were small, the size of marbles. I packed them with enough chi to make them solid but not deadly. I wanted to avoid any senseless death. My killing would be precise and surgical. The Black Lotus and specifically Monique were my targets.

I turned to face the speaker. He was one of the kitchen staff. I could tell from the white uniform and the food stains across his chest.

"Sorry," I said. My voice sounded odd. It had that strange dissonance when Maelstrom took over, but I felt in complete control. The glyphs must have something to do it. He startled and began to get closer.

"Hey, are you okay? You don't sound so good. Did he do something to you? Should I call the boss? She said to report anything strange. I'm gonna call her," he said as he was reaching for something just out of my field of vision.

I raised my hand, signaling I was okay and sent the orbs at him. They each had a small percussive force. Enough to stun but not enough to do major harm. The first one caught him by surprise and sent him off balance. I used two more to knock him out and caught him before he hit the ground. There was a pantry area in the back and I put him in there. Hopefully he would remain out of sight long enough for me to get out of this place. As I turned to leave the pantry I saw the glowing red light. He had flipped a switch before I put him down.

Shit, that can't be good. I looked for the exit and was walking toward it when I saw the figures heading my way. There were three of them. They were dressed like monitors but only two of them approached. I guessed the third for a reader since he was the one who spoke first.

"There he is. Stop him or Monique will have our heads," said the third.

I created more orbs and flung them at the two who were approaching. These men worked for or with Monique, which meant all bets were off. I made the orbs dense but non percussive. It was the equivalent of getting shot with a twelve-gauge shotgun at point-blank range. They both went flying back past the third, dead before hitting the floor. I wanted the third one alive. Grabbing a large knife from the counter, I walked over to the reader.

"You're a reader, aren't you," I said.

149

He nodded.

"Good. You are going to get me out of this place. If you do this I promise you won't die like these two," I said.

"No, I can't. Monique will kill me if I help you," he said and started to step back.

"I can do much worse than Monique, trust me," I said, my voice sounding alien to my ears.

"You don't understand," he said as he turned and ran. I sent several orbs after him slamming him into the wall. He fell to the floor unconscious.

I stood in the kitchen with two bodies on the floor and a large knife in my hand. This didn't look good. I put the knife in one of the robe pockets and left the kitchen through the same door they had come in. She had a real hold over those who worked for her. The readers would be able to find me if they were in proximity. I needed to steer clear of everyone. As I walked down the passageway I noticed how deserted the areas were. The hallway I was in led to a larger junction, connecting to three more hallways. I had no way of knowing which hallway to pick. I was about to take the middle one when I saw the figure walking toward me.

"I don't know how you got out, traitor, but you are going back," he said as he drew a sword.

I sent orbs flying at him and he deflected all of them with a wave of his hand. This was no ordinary monitor. It was a member of the Black Lotus. I would recognize that clothing anywhere.

Maelstrom, I need you to manifest now.

Vessel, I have been manifested since those infernal bands came off. How do you think you are walking around? Do you think your liquid diet was sufficient? I am keeping you upright.

That was a revelation. *I need a weapon.*

Vessel, you are a weapon.

I am a weapon? I was answered with silence. The cryptic answer Maelstrom gave me resonated with something Owl had said. *The weapon does not make the warrior, the warrior makes the weapon. I am the weapon.* It was starting to make sense. I sent chi in to my hand. Focusing it, channeling and directing it. A staff formed. It wasn't Maelstrom, but it would be enough.

The swordsman came at me, lunging. I could see a black aura surrounding his sword and knew it was covered in poison. I created more orbs and sent them. I knew he would deflect them. In fact I counted on it. I followed the orbs in and closed the distance. He would either deflect the orbs and get hit by me or parry my attack and let the orbs hit. I didn't think he could do both. I was right. He chose to let the orbs hit and deal with my attack.

 I hadn't put much energy into the orbs because I had the staff in my hand. They were strong enough to knock him off balance, which I used to my advantage. I rotated my body sideways, avoiding a slash as I struck with the staff, shattering a collarbone. His sword arm was useless. He switched hands but I could see the awkward hold on the sword. He wasn't used to fighting with his off-hand. He attempted a horizontal slash. I stepped in before he began and struck him twice with a spear hand in the throat, crushing his trachea. He fell to the ground grabbing his throat and gasping for breath. He would be gone in a few seconds. I heard footsteps approaching and headed down another corridor. I didn't have time to move the body. I could hear the commotion behind me as I headed down the corridor.

"Sound the alarm. Keep him contained to this section of the dojo grounds. Do not let him get to the main area. Is that understood? Goddammit, how did he get out? Go find him before she gets back and I have to explain how he got loose," said a gruff-sounding voice.

That confirmed that this area was restricted. It could be it was only for Black Lotus. Who was giving the orders? I didn't have time to consider that for long. I needed to get out. At least now I was armed. This presented its own set of problems. How many monitors walked around with weapons in their hands? I could hear footsteps coming my way and prepared myself for a fight when I was grabbed from behind and pulled backwards.

THIRTY-SIX

RAEL STOOD BEFORE THE DOJO on Mott Street. Everything looked quiet from the outside. He had sent the Gyrevex to another location to find a nearby ascendant. They would report back when they found him. Really it was a ploy to be alone. He knew what they were, besides being nearly indestructible weapons of mayhem and chaos. They were Lucius's eyes and ears. Watching him and insuring that he fulfilled his mission. He was tired of being watched.

Long ago he had trained at this dojo, back when he was free and life had meaning. He knew there were ascendants here. He could feel the concentration of power and something else. Hesitating at the door, he cocked his head to one side, homing in on the sensation.

Could I be that lucky? A core ascendant is in there?

He pushed in the door and entered. The fact that the door was open at this hour didn't surprise him. It was a challenge just to find the entrance. The nexus dojo existed partially in the mirror, which made it hard to pinpoint its exact location. If you did manage to find the door by accident there were enough safeguards inside to convince you to leave. Unless you were there to kill ascendants. He had no illusions about completing his mission. The alternative was unthinkable. He passed the reception area. The large wall behind the desk obscured the dojo floor. Walking around the wall and down the narrow hallway, memories flooded back. He remembered the first time he had heard about the Warriors of the Way. He recalled his excitement at being asked to join.

Entering the dojo proper, he could sense something was off. There was an undercurrent of activity. He saw several students running down one of the hallways that led away from the dojo. One of them hung back and Rael caught up to him.

"What's going on?" said Rael.

"Where have you been? There's been a general alarm. Everyone must stay in their areas. Monitors are being summoned to the west wing of the complex," said the student. The student looked at Rael and noticed the swords and the rest of the clothing. "Wait, who are you, again?"

"I'm a visiting instructor, and I'm a little lost," said Rael.

"Yeah, that happens. This place is huge. Lost instructors happen all the time."

He looked around the corridor as if confused. "Can you point me in the right direction? I need to get to my quarters," said Rael.

The student looked at him and sighed.

Rael nodded. *I see not much has changed since my time here.*

"Could you show me where the west wing is so I can avoid it? I don't want to get in anyone's way my first week here," said Rael in a pleasant voice.

The student stopped and showed him the area to avoid.

"If you go down those doors make sure you stay on your right--that will take you to the instructor quarters. Don't head down the left side," said the student and headed off at a brisk pace. "Good luck, I'd better go."

"Thank you again," said Rael. *My luck has been good, indeed.*

He headed down the corridor past the doors and turned left. The activity died down and the corridor was empty for the most part. Rael could sense the increase in chi. It permeated the air. He reached a junction in the corridor where there seemed to be some activity. Two men were standing over a body.

"What happened here?" said Rael. Using an air of authority worked with those lower in the order of the monitors. As long as neither of the men were ranking monitors, Rael could get answers without raising suspicion.

The men answered without turning around. Rael could see they were some kind of forensic team. One took samples of the victim's robe. The other made a point of not touching the sword that lay by his side. Rael could see the Black Lotus poison along its edges.

"Traitor came through here and killed" —he flipped some papers on a clipboard—"it says here 'Geoff' and I can't pronounce this last name," said the first as he pointed at the body. "Where do they find these guys?"

"Usually the bottom of the warrior barrel," said the second.

"Was he skilled?" said Rael.

"He was Black Lotus," said the second. "Those guys are part of the elite team. Yes, he was skilled."

Rael noticed the difference in clothing from the forensic team and the dead man on the ground. The Black Lotus had not changed much since his time. Still wearing black and using poorly trained thugs. The Lotus actually took the dregs from the warrior and guardian groups. They weren't superior fighters but there were enough of them to overwhelm any enemy.

"Obviously not skilled enough. Who is leading the retraction team?" said Rael.

"It's all Black Lotus now. Started with the monitors, but after this…" said the first as he put his samples in a small case. The second put on some gloves and was going to reach for the sword. Rael stopped him.

"I wouldn't touch that if I were you," said Rael.

"I have gloves on, it should be fine," said the second.

"It won't be fine, not unless you prefer going blind right before you die," said Rael. "The entire weapon is covered in poison, even the hilt." He pointed to the Black Lotus on the ground. "They are made immune to it over a long and painful process. It will eat right through those gloves and get in your skin in seconds."

The second forensic team member went back to his pack and grabbed a pair of tongs.

"A much wiser decision. Can you tell me who is heading the Lotus team?"

The first team member answered. "Monique." They both shook their heads. "She gives me the creeps, ever since Diana she's been on a rampage."

"Is this Monique dangerous?"

The two forensic members looked at each other.

"You don't know her?" said the second member. He placed the sword in a metal case.

"It's my first week here…visiting instructor," said Rael.

"If you can help it, steer clear of her," said the first member.

"I'll do that, thanks," said Rael as he left them in the junction.

In moments the Gyrevex would join him. They never stayed away from him for too long. He moved down the corridors looking for more activity. *If I dispatch a core ascendant, it will have an excellent ripple effect that should bring the weapon bearer out of hiding.*

The area was less populated but he managed to see a group of the Lotus gathered ahead. It was another junction. The group was getting orders from a woman. Rael approached as several of the Lotus turned to face him. He didn't need to sense the Gyrevex getting closer, he could hear the screams of those who encountered them.

"Search these halls again. This was his last known position. I don't need to tell you what will happen if he isn't found," said Monique. "And someone go find out what all that screaming is about."

Rael walked up to the group. He could sense the core ascendant was close.

"You have a core ascendant here," said Rael as he drew his swords. Dark energy crackled around him. Some of the Black Lotus that were close to him were hit and sent flung back. Monique's daggers appeared in her hand.

"And you are?" she said as she took a fighting stance.

"My name is Rael, but all my enemies call me the Harbinger."

THIRTY-SEVEN

A HAND KEPT MY MOUTH CLOSED as I was pulled back into a tunnel. I ducked down and threw the person over my hip, holding my staff in front of me. The figure landed gracefully and rolled. He turned to face me, hands up in front of him.

"Dante, it's me," said the figure.

I recognized the voice. It was Devin.

"How do I know you are the real Devin? You could be a trick," I said as I kept the staff in a defensive position.

"I gave you the prism, remember? Think, why would I do that and attack you now? You can't believe the things they told you about us. The box, it wears away at you. They give you manar so you are weak mentally and physically. Everything is true, Dante. Right now Rael is here somewhere looking for you. I can feel him," said Devin.

"How the hell did you survive Roman? I saw you die."

"You saw me get hit repeatedly. I still had enough energy to deflect his hammer. I knew he couldn't unleash its full force in such a closed space, so I only had to deal with the raw impact of the weapon. It was no picnic, trust me," said Devin. "Took me weeks to recover from that fight. He is definitely stronger."

"How did you get away from that place? I don't even know where it was," I said.

"The hall of Sherfym, it's one of the in-between planes. I used retrievers. I had to let him think he had me. It was the only way to get you out of there. Once I saw you were gone I used one of the retrievers on your bed to get myself back here."

It *was* Devin.

"Senpai," I said and sagged against the wall.

He grabbed me and held me up.

"No time for that now. Rael is here and he is looking for you."

I caught my breath as I leaned against the wall. I realized that even Maelstrom had its limits. I shook my head and focused.

"The others, Meja—"

"Are off-plane and you need to get out of here. I don't think you are ready to face the Harbinger yet. Here, take this."

He handed me a small metallic rectangle the size of a business card.

"That is keyed to Meja. Wherever she is it will take you to her," he said.

"They aren't dead?" I said as relief and disbelief overwhelmed me.

"I would know if she were— *she* isn't, at least. I don't know about the others. You need to get to her."

I nodded. *They were alive? I thought I had lost them all. I thought I was alone again.*

"That is an area wide retriever. It works within a fifty-foot circle. Do you know what that means?"

"I should be alone when I use it?"

"Unless you need to move a group, yes you need to be alone to use it," said Devin.

I fingered the small rectangle. It had a small depression in the center just the right size for a fingertip.

"You can't use it in here, too many energies dampening it. Need to get you out of the dojo. Once you are clear you put your thumb in the space and don't remove it, understand? Don't take your finger off of it once in transit."

I heard the words but they didn't register right away. He shook me once.

"Yeah, yes, I got it, finger in depression once I'm out of dojo," I said.

"We need to get out of here. Monique and Rael are about to get at it and I don't think this area of the complex is going to survive that confrontation," said Devin.

He headed down the tunnel and I followed.

"Can she take him?" I said.

"She's strong. He's stronger. He also has Lucius giving him power and an unlimited supply of Gyrevex and those things are impossible to get rid of, you kill one and he gets two more. There must be ten in the complex and they are all heading for Rael now," said Devin as he took several turns and the tunnel dipped and then rose. We came to a dead end.

"I've seen them," I said as the memory of the giants flashed in my mind.

"If you ever have to fight them, remember the neck, throat and eyes are their only weak points. It won't kill them outright but it should make it easier to take them out," he said. "Oh and don't get hit by the bells they carry. It's not pretty."

He was feeling around the surface of the wall as he spoke, until he found the notch he was looking for.

"I haven't used these tunnels in years," he said as he opened a door that led to the dojo complex.

"You go out this door and keep right. It will take you to an exit from the dojo," he said.

He took off a small backpack he was carrying and handed it to me.

"Here you go. Some clothes, money and something you might need," he said.

I changed into my clothes and felt around the backpack until I found the rectangular object at the bottom, Mariko's fan. I tucked it into one of my side pockets.

"I would suggest heading to an open area to use that," he said, pointing at the retriever. "Central Park would be good. Should be far enough from here to avoid any interference and mostly empty at this hour."

"You aren't coming with me?" I said.

"I have to go back. Monique is outclassed. She may be deluded and twisted, but I can't let Rael kill her."

"Why not?" I had no problem with letting Monique get erased by Rael. "She attacked us, poisoned Meja and the rest of us," I said. I could sense the anger surfacing.

"She's been tricked and lied to just like you were. She thought she was hunting and stopping traitors who want to destroy the Warriors of the Way and take over the plane. Can you blame her?"

"Yes I can," I said.

"Moments ago you weren't sure if you could trust me, would you have attacked?"

I thought about it and he was right. I would have attacked him if he hadn't spoken and convinced me.

"I thought so," he said and smiled. "There is one more reason I can't let her die," he said as he pushed me out of the doorway and into the dojo complex.

"What?"

"I'm a Warrior of the Way," he said. "And she's my wife."

"She's your *what*? Are you insane?" I said, incredulous.

"It's complicated. No time to explain now. Get to the others, I'll see you soon," he said as he closed the door.

I could hear him running back. I was in the hallway wearing a reader's robes. I stayed to the right and saw the corridor that would lead to the exit. There was only one small problem. Not all of the Gyrevex were heading toward Rael. The door was blocked by three of them.

THIRTY-EIGHT

THE HEALER LED SYLK TO THE clearing. It was a large stone circle surrounded by trees. In the center of the circle was the mark of the Rah Ven. It looked similar to Grawl's mark, a fang ending in the head of a Rah Ven. With this mark being more intricate. Upon closer inspection Sylk noticed two concentric circles inside the larger stone circle. *This is a tré. Is it still active? It looks intact.* He examined the tré to make sure that each of the circles remained unbroken. *How did a tré get here?*

One of the older Rah Ven stood in the center of the circle. He called both Sylk and Cane to the center of it. His arms and face were covered in scars.

"My name is Arnas and I will be the center of the circle for this ritual," said the old warrior.

He turned to face Cane. "What are the conditions? First blood, concession or death? As challenger it is your choice."

Cane took a moment to assess Sylk. His eyes shone with malice as he spoke. He turned to the assembled Rah Ven.

"I did not wish this outcome, but Grawl, our leader, has left us no choice," said Cane. "He dared to insult us by sending a two-legged as his proxy."

Many in the crowd growled their agreement.

"He has a blood scar, and yes, he bears our mark, but he is not Rah Ven!"

The voices in the crowd were growing louder, agreeing with Cane.

Cane turned to Arnas.

"To uphold my family's honor and the honor of this pack, I choose death," said Cane.

"Death it is," said Arnas. "Let it be noted that this ritual will be to the death. Only one can exit this circle alive," said Arnas.

Arnas turned to Sylk. "What say you, what shall be the weapon?"

Sylk turned to the crowd. Most looked at him with hatred or disgust, some however seemed sympathetic.

"I was sent here by Grawl." *The crafty old dog.* "Because my companions suffered from a poison only the wise Rah Ven had the cure to. He made me give him my word that I would bring the sword to those who hunt Rah Ven young and bind them against their will across the planes. Even if it costs me my life I am sworn to hunt the night shadows," said Sylk.

There were murmurs in the crowd and Sylk could see his words had turned some to his side. Cane looked at him darkly.

Arnas coughed, but looked at him with thinly-veiled admiration. "The weapon?"

"I choose the sword," said Sylk.

"Let it be recorded that the weapon of choice is the sword," said Arnas as two swords were brought to the center of the circle.

"Are you sure you want this weapon, two-legger? I have had many years to practice with a blade," said Cane, grabbing one of the swords from Arnas and executing intricate thrusts and parries. Several in the crowd cheered him on.

"I may not be as old as you, but I have had ample time to learn the craft of fighting with a blade," Sylk said and took the sword that was offered to him.

Sylk took a deep breath and centered himself. He sent his chi deep into the circle beneath him to see if it still had any life. *Inside a tré I have a chance, but he has to try and use his abilities first.* He could feel that the tré was merely dormant from years of disuse. It would take a large expenditure of chi to make it active again, more than he could expend on his own.

Arnas held up his hand to quiet the crowd down.

"Swords to the death," said Arnas. "There are two conditions. Do not leave the circle." He waited until Cane and Sylk acknowledged him. "Neither of you may use a special ability, aside from your wits. Violation of these conditions" —he looked at Cane— "frees the opponent to act as they wish."

Cane looked at Sylk with a smile, and turned his head from side to side, cracking his neck and flexing.

"It's not too late to turn tail and die," said Cane with a grin that exposed his large fangs.

Sylk smiled and faced Cane. He needed to get him angry and unsettled. He wanted him to shift to canine form. It would be enough to reenergize the circle.

"Tell me, Cane, where were you when they were taking the young? A strong fighter like you, I would think you could take several of the night shadows on your own," said Sylk. "Unless of course you fear them?"

"I fear nothing," said Cane with a growl.

They were circling each other now. Sylk could see his words were having the desired effect.

"If you don't fear them and you didn't stop them that only leaves one explanation. You're working with them. You are helping the night shadows take the young. How much do they give you?" said Sylk. He could see the anger reach Cane's eyes.

"I'll kill you, you filthy two-legger," said Cane as he leapt forward.

Their swords clashed as Sylk barely managed stop the downward slash.

He's relying on his strength and speed. Can't match him in that. Sylk twisted his body and wrapped a foot around Cane's causing him to stumble past. *Have to make him lose face.* "Did they promise you the pack?"

The crowd had gone silent at hearing Sylk's words. Many were wondering silently what Sylk was voicing in the circle.

"No one gives me the pack, I take what is rightfully mine!" yelled Cane.

He lunged at Sylk, slashing. Sylk could see the skill and avoided one slash by a fraction of an inch. The second slash caught him in the arm and drew blood. Cane grinned. It was a feral, malicious thing.

Sylk ignored the cut. "How are you going to lead the pack? You can't even protect the young. Why should they trust you? You're nothing but a mangy half-breed," said Sylk.

 Cane screamed and tossed the sword to one side. Sylk had never seen the human form to Rah Ven transformation occur. Cane's bones popped and cracked as they elongated to shift into the new form. His spine lengthened and his legs and arms changed to support the increase in weight. His hands changed into paws with large claws. His face grew longer and his fangs elongated. Hair grew in an astounding rate all over Cane's body, covering him completely. In human form Cane was impressive— as a Rah Ven he was frightening. He stood taller than any Rah Ven Sylk had encountered. His yellow eyes shone with hatred and promised violence.

"Let's dispense with the pretense, two-legger. I'm going to rip you in two and feast on your entrails," said Cane.

Sylk could feel the circle thrum beneath him. The tré was active again.

"Anywhere else, I would agree. But here, today, in this circle, you have met your end," said Sylk.

With a thought Sylk sent his chi into the outer ring of the circle, causing a barrier to shoot up, enclosing them.

THIRTY-NINE

THE CORRIDOR WAS DESERTED. It would seem the Gyrevex were there to make sure no one left the complex. *I need to get outside.* They hadn't noticed me yet. *Maybe I could just find another way out.* I turned to head in the other direction. My body jerked to the side as a bell crashed into the wall where I stood a second before.

Vessel, you cannot fight them like this and I cannot help you more than I am. Your only recourse is to run.

I was tired of running.

I'm not running any more, I said.

You've grown tired of living, then? I trust my new vessel will live a longer life than you, said Maelstrom.

I turned to face the Gyrevex.

I'm not dying here either. We need to get outside. Ascendants are dying and I have to stop it, I said. *Give me everything you have.*

I told you, that would kill—

Give it to me now.

Very well. It has been my greatest displeasure knowing you, said Maelstrom.

I felt the increase of energy in my body as a swirling black vortex of chi surrounded me. I still held my staff, but it was smoldering. Red energy wafted up from it as the glyphs in my arms pulsed a deep crimson. My nostrils filled with the smell of burning clothes. My vision grew tight and it felt like my skin was too tight on my body.

Maelstrom was right. If I didn't stop this soon it would kill me. I could feel the damage to my body as I remained in the vortex. It was unmaking me, swallowing me into itself. I was dying as I ran at the Gyrevex.

*****

Rael turned suddenly. *The weapon bearer, here?* He turned back to face Monique, his attention divided.

"I would love to dance with you, but it seems the person I'm looking for is calling me," he said as he stepped back from her.

Two Gyrevex stepped in between them.

"I would hate to leave you without a dance partner. Accept my apologies. If you survive, we will meet again, I'm sure," he said as he signaled the Gyrevex.

Monique moved back, keeping a defensive stance as the Gyrevex materialized their bells.

"What the hell is that?" said Monique under her breath.

"Kill her. I don't want her or the Black Lotus interfering. Make sure they don't," he said as he ran off toward the sensation that was tugging at him.

*****

The first Gyrevex came at me. This had been the one that tried to turn me into paste a minute ago. Another bell came at me. I rolled under it and closed the distance with the first Gyrevex. Sidestepping a swipe of its large hand, I buried my staff in its chest. On its way down I materialized a blade in my hand, leaving the smoldering staff buried in the Gyrevex and removed its head.

Two more bells came at me, but the vortex was strong enough to throw them off course and they ended up going past me. As the chains came in contact with the vortex they disintegrated, allowing the bells to continue their trajectory and they crashed into the walls behind me.

I stepped to the second Gyrevex. This one was expecting me. It launched a flurry of attacks. I jumped back, away from a kick and dodged punches that would have done serious damage had they connected. My sword seemed to not affect it even though I cut it many times over. A bell appeared in its hand. I could hear the whirr of the second bell being spun by the third Gyrevex. They were going to attack at the same time.

Those are chi weapons. Let them come, said Maelstrom.

I stood still as the Gyrevex launched both bells at me. The vortex flared with hints of red in the black. As the bells entered the vortex, I could see them disintegrate. I leapt up higher than I should have been able to and catapulted off one of the side walls past the second Gyrevex, slicing its neck as I did so. The third Gyrevex charged. I feinted a dodge left and slid right. I was fast, much faster than it. When it tried to correct its direction of attack I was there waiting. I sliced across its neck and watched it fall to the ground.

Behind me, someone was clapping.

FORTY

THE BARRIER CLOSED THE CIRCLE, creating a semi-opaque dome that enclosed the space and rose fifty feet in the air. The crowd stepped back in surprise. A few of Cane's pack mates attempted to push against the barrier. Sylk could hear the screams and smell the burning skin.

"This will only make your death swift, two-legger," said Cane as he circled Sylk. Sylk stood in the center. He had no need to turn and face Cane. Inside a tré his senses were heightened and he could 'see' every inch of the circle without his eyes. He summoned a shield of orbs. Each one was an inch in diameter and floated in lazy circles around him.

Cane shimmered and disappeared using his camouflage. Sylk expected this. He spread out the trajectory of the orbs and sped them up. The first one collided with Cane as he tried to attack. The impact rocked him back into view. He landed on his hind legs, lost his balance and fell into the barrier. Cane stepped away from the barrier, his fur singed where it had touched him.

"Your cheap tricks won't stop me," said Cane.

"Tell me, Cane, what were you offered?" said Sylk.

"Shut your filthy mouth," growled Cane.

Sylk stepped close and the pendant around his neck began to glow with a subdued white light. Cane swiped at him and missed, hitting an orb. The explosion threw him on his side. Sylk could see the blood flowing from the paw. Sylk ran in and stabbed him as he lay on the ground. Cane howled.

"You *will* tell me before I end you. What was the nature of your agreement with the night shadows?" said Sylk as he stabbed again.

Blood flowed freely into the circle now. Cane shimmered but did not disappear, Sylk was too close and the pendant interfered with the camouflage. Sylk avoided a lunge and a snap of the jaws that would

174

have removed his leg. He brought down his sword on Cane's head and sent more orbs into him. These didn't explode, but punctured Cane's body. None of the orbs exited his body. Cane lay on his side by the edge of the circle. His breathing was ragged and drool flowed from his jaws.

"You thought I was defenseless like the young you sold," said Sylk as he walked to the center of the circle.

"You think you can stop them? They are the night. They will kill you," said Cane. He stood up and began running at Sylk and froze time. Sylk with a thought detonated all of the orbs inside Cane's body. A few seconds later Cane's bloody body crashed to the ground, missing a leg and gasping for breath.

Sylk approached the dying Rah Ven as he dropped the barrier around the circle. There were gasps from the crowd but no one moved as Arnas stepped into the circle.

"How did you know?" said Cane.

Cane turned his head and looked at Sylk. The metallic smell of blood filled the air.

"I didn't know," said Sylk as he raised his sword. "I said those words to provoke you.

Cane laughed and coughed up blood.

"Well done, two-legger," he rasped. "Finish it."

"My name is Sylk," said Sylk as he brought the sword down, ending Cane's life.

"The rite of acceptance is complete, said Arnas, grabbing Sylk's arm and raising it. "The victor!" There were cheers. Sylk looked into the crowd and noticed that not all were cheering. One group looked ready to jump into the circle and attack. *Those would be his pack mates. Will have to keep an eye on them.*

"That was impressive, Blood Sylk," said a voice from the crowd.

Sylk knew the voice and turned to face the speaker. A wave of energy preceded the speaker as he drew closer. The Rah Ven parted as the figure strode into view.

"While you're here playing with these dogs, the Harbinger is killing ascendants in the hub and the barrier between planes is failing," said the figure.

The speaker stepped forward to hard stares from the crowd and entered the circle. Sylk took a step back. He could feel the overwhelming flow of chi as it left Roman and flowed into the circle beneath them.

"Roman. What do you want?" said Sylk.

"Balance, Sylk, My job is to restore balance and in order to do that I need the core ascendant. I thought he would be with you or the monitor but it appears she is indisposed and he is not here," said Roman. His large hammer hung from his back. *He's been to see the healer.*

"Did you kill them?" said Sylk.

"What kind of monster do you take me for? I only need the core, alive. Of course I didn't kill them," said Roman.

"I don't know where he is— as you said, I have been busy here," said Sylk. He kept his voice calm. *I don't want to set him off. That would mean a massacre.*

Roman nodded and murmured something under his breath.

"Aurora will not be pleased, Sylk, if she gets directly involved in this…"

"Please convey my apologies to your mistress. Once I find him I will be certain to communicate that to her or you," said Sylk.

"No need, Sylk, I will find him. I found you"—he turned to face the Rah Ven—"even here. I will find him. Stay out of my way, Karashihan. I would hate to have to kill you," he said as he opened a portal and vanished from the circle.

FORTY-ONE

I TURNED AROUND TO SEE THE Harbinger giving me a golf clap and blocking the exit.

"A core ascendant *and* the weapon bearer, you are *full* of surprises," he said as he drew his swords.

"Stay away. I don't think I can control it anymore," I said.

The vortex continued to swirl around me, red and black. I could see that it was dissolving the wall to either side of me.

"That's because it's not yours— you need to return the weapon. It doesn't belong to you," he said.

"It's mine now," I said.

Energy arced from his swords into the floors and walls causing scorch marks wherever it hit. The dim light of the hallway made it hard to make out his expression.

"Are you strong enough to kill me?" he said. "Before it kills you?"

"I need to get outside. I need to get to the others. Get out of my way," I said.

"You're dead anyway. Why prolong the inevitable? Let me end you and take the weapon back to my master. That way we all win," he said as he closed the distance. I could see he noticed the glyphs on my arms. They were hard to miss, glowing the way they were.

"What the hell are those?" he pointed at my forearms. "Wait, don't tell me. They put suppression shackles on you, didn't they?" he said, incredulous.

"Custom made," I said as I raised my arm.

"And you got free how...oh no. You used the weapon, didn't you," he said.

"It was the only way," I said.

"The only way? You idiot! The weapon is bonded to you now. I can't remove it from you now even if I wanted to, even if death came and claimed you herself. I couldn't help you. Only he can take it from you now," he said.

"Who?" I said.

"I can't let you die. Goddammit, things can never be simple. Fine, I can take you to him near death— alive is all that matters," he said as he attacked.

I still had the sword in my hand and brought it up to protect myself as his swords came at me. The arcing energy from his swords was being absorbed by the vortex around me. I could feel the surge in power as it drained the swords of energy.

"You can't stop me," I said as I felt myself losing my grip on everything. "No one can." I started laughing.

"I don't need to stop you, I just need to give you enough energy and you will do it for me," he said as we locked swords.

The vortex swirled on, unmaking me. It seemed to have little outward effect on him. He must have seen the surprise register on my face as he stepped into the destructive force.

"I'm harder to kill than most," he said as he let one sword disintegrate and grabbed my hand.

He began to send energy in every direction as the vortex grew around us. His other sword was being dismantled by the vortex. In seconds, it too would be gone. I could see him begin to trace symbols with his free hand.

Behind me I could sense Devin getting closer. Behind him I could 'see' Monique and a group of monitors closing in on us. I pushed back and tried to break contact with Rael. His grip was too strong. I managed to push his sword to the side. He was so focused on the symbols he was tracing he didn't see my attack until it was too late. My sword entered his neck as a portal opened beneath us.

"Dante, no!" yelled Devin. It was too late.

"That should do it," said Rael as he fell to the ground.

He wasn't distracted. He let me attack him. My attack unleashed more chi than I ever thought possible. The portal flared and I began falling. I turned in time to see Devin and the rest flung to the walls by the backlash of the chi wave. Then my vision went white.

FORTY-TWO

"HOW LONG BEFORE THEY are ready to move?" said Sylk.

He had gone straight to the healer's home after Roman left the circle. Fearing the worst, he entered and found the group undisturbed with the healer tending to the beds. Mara and Kal were standing guard as he came in. He told them about the ritual and was anxious to get back to the hub, especially after seeing Roman.

"This is not a fast process. Blood flow must be controlled. Too much and they can become part Rah Ven, too little and they die," said the healer.

"Humans can become part Rah Ven?" said Kal.

"It's where all the stories of werewolves come from," said Mara. "Rah Ven are the source."

"Werewolves, bah! Pretty name for an ugly creature. Rah Ven blood mingled with human, it creates one of those— things. Not human and not Rah Ven. Something in between," said the healer.

"Does that mean…" said Kal as she looked at the beds.

The healer slammed her hand on the table. The sound filled the small room, bouncing off the walls.

"I be here to control the flow. No one can question that. I be the one to make sure the flow is correct and no harm comes to them as best I can," said the healer.

"We do not doubt your abilities, grandmother," said Sylk. "I just feel we have been here too long. We have urgent matters in the hub." *How are we going to stop Roman and Rael? Where are you, Dante?*

She seemed to calm down after Sylk spoke to her.

"More urgent than your friends surviving?" said the healer.

Sylk remained silent as he looked out the window.

"What about Zen?" said Kal. "He doesn't look good."

"The large one?" said the healer, nodding. "Yes, the poison is running fierce in him. Even with extra blood, his outcome is a question. Only the flow can help him now."

"And the others?" said Sylk.

"One more day, one more day should suffice," said the healer.

"We can do one more day if we have no choice," said Sylk.

"None. Come with me, alpha," she said as she went to the back room where the beds were. She closed the door behind them, keeping the others out.

"We need to talk private. The big one is worse off than the rest. The flow won't help him," she said.

"You said—"

"I only said what I said because the girl is fond of him, but it's not going well for him."

"Is he going to die?"

"The poison did too much damage. I can't bring him back to the way he was before, but I can let the Rah Ven blood mix with his, making him one of those things…"

"A werewolf," said Rah Ven.

She waved a hand dismissively at his comment.

"We have a place for them here where he can live until he accepts his new blood," she said.

"Will he be safe?" said Sylk.

"He will be part Rah Ven and he will have life, but he must stay here for his first year to manage the change. It's that or death. This is your choice as alpha."

"I choose life," said Sylk. *The warrior will need a new guardian.*

She pressed her lips together and nodded, adjusting the vials and flow of blood in Zen's bed.

"It's best if they think he has passed from the poison. He will not be able to be part of that life again," said the healer.

"You mean lie to them," said Sylk.

"I will do it. You are the alpha now. This is not your task. This life will be soft lies to hold back the hard truths for the good of the pack," she said.

"Grandmother," said Sylk. "What of the pack now? Not all were pleased with the outcome of the ritual."

"Cane's dogs." She spat to the side. "You speak wisdom. They will want revenge. You must deal with them soon or they will splinter the whole. They won't act so close to Cane's defeat in the circle. Cowards like that will wait until you are not watching, striking when they think you are weak. You must not show weakness in dealing with them. Like bad blood they must be removed before they poison the whole," she said.

"Like Cane," said Sylk.

"I will shed no tears for that one. Rotten to the core. I don't know about this night shadow business they tell me you accused him of, but he was a bad one, evil. We're better off with him gone," she said.

"Grawl is a crafty one," said Sylk. His eyes were feeling heavy.

"That he is. You are the leader for Grawl now," she said, pointing at Sylk. "Duly done by ritual and blade. Until Grawl comes back and takes his rightful place, you speak and act as leader of the pack."

Sylk nodded. *Did Grawl see this far ahead? I will have to ask him when we meet again.* He sat down on one of the unoccupied beds, and rested his head, letting it sink into one of the pillows. The healer stood and put a hand on his lap.

"Rest a moment, I will do this," she said as she left for the other room. The smell of blood permeated the room, coppery and pungent. Even after all this time he could smell a capful in a large room. Rah Ven or human, it was the same. The smell was familiar, like an old shirt. *So much blood in his lifetime, on and off the battlefield. I am never far away from the blood.*

He could hear the healer in the other room and Kal's cry.

"No, no, *you* said he would pull through," said Kal.

The pain and loss were clear in Kal's voice. She had lost her sister and now this. He could hear the healer's soothing voice and Kal's sobs.

Soft lies for hard truths. Life is blood and blood is life.

He was just closing his eyes when Samir awoke with a yell, startling him. Sylk went over to the syllabist as the healer entered the room.

"What is it, Samir, are you in pain?" said Sylk.

The healer began to adjust the liquids and Samir began to drift off. He gripped Sylk's hand with surprising strength.

"Karashihan, the warrior— the warrior is gone," said Samir as he drifted back into unconsciousness.

FORTY-THREE

THE VORTEX WAS GONE. I stood in a rock garden. I could just make out the details of the garden as my eyes began to adjust when a fist crashed against the side of my head, sending me reeling.

"That was for the sword in the throat. Be thankful I don't just return the favor," said Rael. "I brought him here. He's all yours now. I have ascendants to kill."

I found one of the benches at the edge of the garden and sat down, rubbing my face.

"You'll have to forgive him," said the figure that appeared next to me causing me to jump off the bench. "He hates it when I bring him back. I think one day I will give him his wish and let him die, just not today."

The old man sat very still and looked at me. His storm-cloud gray eyes pierced right through me. His white hair was long and drawn back into a braid. His slender build radiated strength and power. He wore a simple gray robe that matched the color of his eyes. His hands were lost in the folds of his sleeves. I was looking at Sylk's ancestor, Lucius.

"Are you Lucius the destroyer?" I said.

He laughed. It was a pleasant sound that filled the garden.

"You have something that belongs to me, warrior," he said.

I searched within to see if I could feel Maelstrom, but felt nothing.

"Don't bother. You won't feel any chi in this place," he said.

"Who are you?"

"The real question is, who are you? Haven't you ever wondered how you ended up with your weapon? A weapon designed to cause massive death and destruction?"

"The weapon doesn't make the warrior, the warrior makes the weapon," I said.

"Ah, my old friend Owl. He betrayed me in the end, when I counted on him the most. I see he has moved on and yet a part of him remains, in you. If you believe that, what kind of warrior are you? Did you pick the weapon or did it pick you?"

"Sylk accelerated the process of my manifestation. That was the reason Maelstrom picked me," I said, my words uncertain.

"Sylk. Did you know he is my distant relative and yet even now plots against me? Where is the family loyalty? No, warrior, he facilitated your manifestation but you picked. He opened the door but you walked in. You picked the weapon— my weapon."

"Who are you?" *I needed to hear it.*

"I am the owner of the weapon you possess or that now possesses you. My name is Lucius Iman, first in the house of Iman, chief among the wavedancers and first of the Karashihan," he said.

"Are you removing your weapon?" I felt it was an important question given the circumstances.

"My weapon is bonded to you, which makes extricating it difficult. If I kill you it will merely return to the void and await another vessel. I cannot access the void from here. Which means I must remove it from you while you are alive," he said.

"How?"

"I will coax the weapon out by threatening your life," he said.

We began to walk the garden. I could hear birds singing in the trees. Along the path, the cherry blossoms were in in bloom, their petals a soft pink against a blue sky. The aroma wafted over us, reminding me of roses.

"Why do you need it?"

"Maelstrom is a tool, one of three foci my family created. With it I can locate the other two and continue what I started before I was exiled here. Before the order of warriors betrayed me and my family."

"I was told you betrayed them," I said. *I don't know who to believe.*

"By Owl, no doubt. History is written by the victors, warrior. Did he tell you why they were so determined to wipe out my family?"

"He said you were the first Karashihan but decided to be a warrior with two guardians," I said.

"Decided? I was *assigned* two guardians to be my 'escorts' wherever I went. The abilities of my bloodline were deemed too powerful. Wavedancers do not need to enter the mirror to use their ability. We can listen through surfaces as well. At the very head of the Order I uncovered corruption. The Warriors of the Way were being led by corrupt Samadhi. Do you know this term?" he said.

I nodded. "Samadhi are the masters of the respective disciplines within the order of the Warriors of the Way."

"Correct. Each discipline must have three masters to ensure the knowledge is never lost," he said. "I was beyond the Samadhi in my discipline. When I uncovered their plan to subjugate the planes, I took action."

"Subjugate the planes? How?"

"How many planes have a Watch now?"

"Every plane has a presence of the order. We keep the planes safe from our enemies."

"Which enemies?"

I remained silent. So far the enemies I had were the Black Lotus and the warriors sent after me. Even Roman wasn't out to kill or imprison me like the Lotus had done.

"I saw with my own eyes the atrocities committed by the Order on the outer planes, the ones not directly connected to the hub. When I confronted my peers, I was called unstable. The power had gone to my head, they said. They secretly sent the newly formed Black Lotus after my family, murdered them in their sleep. In their beds. My wife. My children. They tried to eradicate my entire bloodline. They took everything from me, men and women I had trusted with my life. That was when I began to kill Samadhi."

His voice had grown thick as he recalled the memories.

"How did you end up here?" I said.

"Some of the Lotus had fled to these outer planes. I gave chase. My hatred knew no bounds. They had killed my family, warrior. I did not know this was a trap. Once in the outer plane, they severed the connection to the hub plane, stranding this triad. Once I was stranded, my abilities diminished. They placed suppressor bracelets on me and purged me of my chi, causing me to lose my weapon. You now sit in the lost triad," he said.

"How did they sever the connection?" *The longer I keep him talking the longer I have to figure a way out.*

"The hub is the source of chi to the planes. It radiates outward from there. Each plane has its own source of chi that is augmented by the hub source. As long as you are connected to the hub you will feel no measurable difference in your ability. Once cut from the hub, it will feel like you have lost your chi," he said.

He turned to face me then, his gray eyes measuring me. His face was tranquil. A man at peace with his decision.

"Have you made your peace? It's probable you will not survive the purging," he said.

I dug deep, searching for any sensation of Maelstrom or chi.

"It's futile, warrior. It took me many decades to reconnect to my source of chi in this place. Bring him to the tré," he said.

Two Gyrevex appeared beside me and grabbed my arms. I couldn't resist them as they half dragged me to a clearing on the other side of the garden. In the center of the clearing was a tré about thirty feet across. A deep golden glow emanated from the three concentric circles. He waited for me in the center as the Gyrevex dropped me beside him. They wafted into smoke as a barrier rose up along the outer circle.

191

"This is unfortunate. Like the ascendants. They must die to reestablish the connection to the hub. You must die to return my weapon. I wish there were another way, warrior."

I realized there was no point in trying to convince him otherwise. He had spent decades trapped in this place. His plan was set and there was no deviating from it. I stood before him, realizing how powerless I was. There was nothing I could do to defend myself. He extended an arm toward me as if signaling me to stop, and my world exploded. The center of the tré was bathed in golden light. I was suspended midair in the light. The first sensation was heat, unbearable heat, burning me inside and out. Then came the lancing pain. It felt as if my intestines were being ripped out inch by inch. I doubled over, screaming in agony. The pain travelled up my chest and into my throat, suffocating me. My screams were cut off as I struggled to breathe.

"He is ready. Position him," I heard Lucius say.

My arms were grabbed and extended to the sides. I could see the Gyrevex out of the corner of my eyes but I couldn't turn my head. Lucius had his arms raised and brought them both down to his sides. A bolt of energy hit the top of my head. The impact was staggering. I could feel the blood run down my eyes, nose, ears and the metallic taste filled my mouth. The vortex formed and flowed out of me. The

Gyrevex were dissolved in seconds, but I remained in place, their job done.

I could see the energy coalescing in front of Lucius. A sphere around two feet in diameter coruscating black, red and gold floated before him. The gold was tethered to me.

"Still you try and thwart me, Owl?" said Lucius.

With a downward slice of his hand he cut off the gold tether and it raced back into my body.

"Pointless, old friend. He is going to die and I have the weapon," he said

He raised a hand and absorbed the sphere in front of him. The black and red energy entered his body and he arched his back as it enveloped him.

"I am whole," he said.

The energy flared around him once and disappeared. A double-bladed short staff appeared in his hand the next moment, Maelstrom. My body remained suspended in the light as he drew closer to me. The crimson and black of Maelstrom radiated in his hand. His gray eyes now had flecks of crimson and black in the irises. He stepped toward my broken body. I felt the waves of chi wash over me as he closed the distance.

"This was your purpose, warrior. You existed to bring this back to me," he said as he lifted Maelstrom to my face. "And now your usefulness has ended."

He pulled back the staff and began to deliver the killing blow when the tré was converted into a crater, flinging me across the garden into the trees. Lucius leapt back, holding Maelstrom before him, bisecting the energy wave and landing on his feet untouched. A huge hammer rested in the center of what used to be the tré.

"Not yet it hasn't. My mistress has a use for him," said a voice. "Go tend to him," he said to the blue clad figures surrounding the crater.

It was Roman.

FORTY-FOUR

"WHAT DID HE MEAN 'gone', Master?" said Mara.

Sylk turned to the healer who was still adjusting the liquids in the other beds.

"Bring him back," said Sylk.

"No, he needs to heal and he can't take the blood while awake," she said.

"This is important," said Sylk.

She moved close to Sylk and poked his chest with her gnarled finger.

"You may be the alpha. In here I am the last word. You heed?" she said, punctuating the end of each sentence with a poke.

"I understand. In that case I need to go see someone," said Sylk.

"Go see whoever you need to see." She went back to her vials. "Just don't bring disturbance to this house," she said added.

Sylk stepped outside and made his way to the clearing with the tré. He needed to form a portal to the Watch. He was still fatigued from the ritual and the added power of the circle would help. He stepped into the circle and traced the symbols. A light silver trail followed his hands as they formed before him. A portal opened a few seconds later. He stepped through, leaving the plane of Rah Ven behind.

In the trees a pair of eyes watched.

Sylk appeared in the courtyard near the obelisk, which had been repaired but was still nonfunctional. He could see the reconstruction had begun. In one of the clearings he saw Rin and made his way over to him.

"Karashihan, it's good to see you," said Rin.

"Where's the Keeper?"

"I don't keep track of his movements—"

"Where is he?" said Sylk. He was growing weary of the manipulations.

"What's this about?" said Rin.

"I can answer that — isn't that why you came, Karashihan?" said the Keeper from behind them.

Rin jumped back but Sylk remained unfazed as he turned to face the Keeper.

"What happened to the warrior?" said Sylk "The syllabist said he was gone. Is he dead?"

"Walk with me, Karashihan, we have much to discuss and these words are not for all ears," said the Keeper as he headed off, staff in hand. Sylk caught up to the old man in a few strides.

"I hear you are a pack leader now," said the Keeper.

Sylk remained silent.

"Grawl will want to speak to you before you leave."

"Leave? Leave where?" said Sylk.

"It would seem that the warrior has been taken to the lost triad," said the Keeper.

Sylk stopped midstride. "Impossible. That triad has been disconnected for over a hundred years. The energy expenditure required to open a portal there would be immense."

"Much longer than that. And yet there it is. The warrior is there and you must go there as well."

"How? The obelisk is destroyed. I used a tré and it took all I had to get here," said Sylk.

"Come see me when you are done with Grawl," said the Keeper as he headed back to the construction.

196

Sylk searched the area for the elder Rah Ven, knowing the Keeper bringing him this way was not a coincidence. He found him on the edges of the Watch tending to the graves of the fallen.

Sylk walked up to the Rah Ven and waited while the group laid their brethren to rest on a series of pyres. Grawl in human form took a torch and lit each one. Sylk counted twenty. After each one was blazing, Grawl came over to Sylk, his face somber.

"Peace, Karashihan," he said.

"Peace, Ancient One," said Sylk.

"I am afraid there will be little of that in the coming days. The destroyer has regained his instrument of death," said Grawl.

"And the warrior?"

"He lives still, for how long I cannot see."

"Are you certain?" said Sylk. *If this is true it means Dante is stripped of Maelstrom. He should be dead and yet he is alive somehow?*

"I am Rah Ven. This is not a soft lie. We speak plain among the pack leaders," said Grawl.

"You used me," said Sylk.

"I set you on a path."

"A path you knew would lead to a meeting with Cane. In a tré. How did a tré get there?"

"The circle of claws does not belong to any one people. Many planes have circles like this," said Grawl. "I knew one day the Rah Ven too would need this circle."

"I cannot lead Rah Ven. I am not Rah Ven," said Sylk as he began taking off the pendant.

Grawl stopped him, placing his hand on the pendant and keeping it in place.

"You are my voice and my hands while I remain here. You are Rah Ven, by blood and blade. No one will contest that. Do not forget your purpose. Stop the hunters of our young. Root out the cancer that lies in my people. I am too old now. My fangs and claws are not as sharp as they once were."

Grawl paused and looked out into the endless sand.

"Soon I will head out into the desert for the last time. When the time comes, a new pack leader will arise and my people will be strong again. You will make sure of this, I have seen it," said Grawl.

Sylk remained silent a moment and then faced away from the pyres to look out into the desolation of the desert.

"I cannot escape the blood, Ancient One," he whispered.

"You cannot escape what you are. Accept it and be free," said Grawl. "You must go now. Run long and run fast, Karashihan."

"Long days to you, Ancient One," said Sylk as the Rah Ven shimmered and disappeared.

Sylk continued looking out into the desert as the Keeper materialized beside him.

"Are you ready?" said the Keeper.

"How is the warrior still alive? Everything is lost if the destroyer has regained the weapon," said Sylk.

"And yet we are still here. Go and make sure it remains that way," said the Keeper.
His staff began to glow with a white light, matching the lines in Sylk's arm.

"Time to go," he said and touched the staff to Sylk's chest, sending him to the lost triad.

FORTY-FIVE

I DON'T KNOW HOW I didn't break every bone in my body as I rag-dolled across the garden. I saw three figures in blue come at me and was helpless to do anything. Any signal I gave my limbs to move was short-circuited by intense pain. They carried me over to another part of the garden and began to heal me. I could see the crater and Roman as he picked up his hammer.

"It's only a matter of time now," said Lucius. "My Harbinger will destroy the remaining ascendants and the barrier will fall."

Maelstrom pulsed in his hand. The blades had grown in size and were almost the size of the staff.

"The barrier hasn't fallen yet. Perhaps he can't find them? It appears your Harbinger is failing you," said Roman.

"What have you done?" said Lucius.

"The remaining ascendants are under Aurora's protection. Your Harbinger will not find them such easy targets. Or it could be his heart is not up to this task. Perhaps the yoke is too tight," said Roman.

"No tighter than yours, and yet you serve your mistress willingly," said Lucius. "Why not join me? Together we can purge the planes of this infestation of warriors."

"I serve my mistress by choice. Did you give your Harbinger a choice?" said Roman as he began to spin his hammer.

"Choice? Choice is for the weak. Where was my choice when my family was butchered? My little ones' broken bodies cast across my home like so much discarded rubbish? My wife murdered protecting them? What choice was given to them?" said Lucius as a vortex formed around him.

"All must pay for the crimes of few?"

"The corruption still exists, enforcer. The Order of the Warriors will be erased," said Lucius.

Even from this distance I could feel the energy emanating from the both of them. The figures had restored my body and I felt almost normal again. I couldn't feel my chi, but my body didn't feel like a raw open wound either. I started to make my way toward Lucius. One of the figures grabbed me by the arm and stopped me.

"You cannot," she said.

"I have to," I said. *I feel different somehow.*

"You will die."

"What's your name?" I said.

"Adra, daughter of Aurora."

"Adra, if I die here, you tell them I tried," I said.

She stepped back and nodded as I ran to the crater.

What the hell am I doing? This is certain death.

Behind me I could hear footsteps matching mine. *Are Roman's people following me?*

I turned and saw a familiar face. Gray eyes took me in, assessing me in seconds. He held a gleaming white sword in his left hand. His right arm was laced with silver lines that shone brightly.

"It looks as if you are racing to your death, warrior. Would you mind some company?" said Sylk.

"Not at all," I said as we headed to the crater.

"Make sure you stay in the crater. It may be partially destroyed, but it is still a tré. There is latent power there," he said as five Gyrevex materialized around us. "Go, I will deal with these."

I rolled under a bell that would have removed my head. Sylk unleashed a barrage of orbs that drew their attention. *How is he accessing chi?*

Then I understood. The circle Roman had partially destroyed had released its power. That was the source of chi in this plane. I reached the edge of the circle and power coursed through my body. It wasn't my chi. This was raw power flowing in every direction. I let it fill me and time slowed. Behind me Sylk was moving in an intricate dance of death as bells flew by him, missing him by fractions of an inch as he dispatched the Gyrevex. One would fall only to have another take its place seconds later.

"Dante, I will deal with the shadow, but you must cut off the source of its power. I cannot do both."

It was Roman. He had joined me at the edge of the circle as vortices spun off from the main one surrounding Lucius.

"Shadow? That isn't Lucius?" I said, unbelieving.

"The destroyer is two planes away from this one. This is his shadow. We could not stand before the first Karashihan so easily."

I looked around at the destruction. I remembered the power of the tré as he stripped Maelstrom from me with a gesture, and this was his shadow.

"He is fearsome, yes? Even as a shadow his power eclipses most," said Roman and then he began laughing. He turned serious and looked at me, putting an arm on my shoulder. "I don't wish to die today. Go to the center of the circle and tap into the power. Cut off the source or this will be the last day any of us see."

He launched himself into the air to avoid the vortex and dove for Lucius's shadow.

He is insane. I ran to the center of the circle without a clue about what I needed to do.

You need a focus. Use the power from the circle to manifest a weapon. Hurry, warrior.

It was Owl.

I stood in the center and the power coursed through me. I stilled my breathing and focused. In the air above me I could hear Roman and the shadow of Lucius clash. Behind me Sylk dodged a bell, cut the chain and removed a Gyrevex while another materialized behind him. Beyond that I could feel the sun on my skin and the wind in the air. I could sense the trees in the garden and the soft blooms of the cherry blossoms as the petals fell to the ground. A golden staff formed itself in my hands and I drove it end-first into the center of the circle.

"You insignificant mote of dust, what are you doing?" said shadow Lucius as he came at me. Roman intercepted him, cutting off his attack. He swung his hammer as shadow Lucius planted his feet next to mine and met the hammer with Maelstrom. It sounded like a tuning fork amplified a thousand times. The force of energy around me was overwhelming.

From the center of the circle a rush of wind gusted, threatening to sweep me off my feet. I gripped the staff with both hands, my knuckles white. The roar was deafening. All of the energy initially dispersed by Roman's hammer strike began to coalesce in the staff, making it glow.

Don't let go, warrior.

The Gyrevex began to fall and disappear. The last Gyrevex disintegrated and Sylk ran over to where Roman was attacking shadow Lucius.

I held on, but had to look away as the wind buffeted me. The intensity of the light from the staff kept increasing. My face felt sunburned and it blinded me even with my eyes closed. It wasn't just the chi from the tré that was filling the staff. All the chi from the plane was being siphoned in. I sensed when all the trees around the garden began to wither and die. The once fertile soil turned to dust and began to swirl around, lifeless. The relentless wind uprooted them and flung them away. In moments I was in the center of a wasteland, and still the energy flowed in.

Prepare yourself, warrior.

Sylk had closed the distance, his gleaming sword thrusting in while Roman slammed his hammer to the ground. The amount of energy they sent my way didn't register compared to energy flowing from the staff I held onto.

Shadow Lucius thrusted with Maelstrom, burying it in Sylk's leg and driving him to one knee. Lucius laughed and I could hear the familiar dissonance in his voice.

"I will make sure you suffer. You will beg me for death, progeny, and I will deny you," said Lucius.

Roman brought his hammer around for a killing blow and Lucius stopped it with his other hand. He was still laughing as he began to force Roman's hammer down to the ground while driving the blade of Maelstrom in to Sylk's leg.

Now, warrior. You must strike.

I removed the staff from the ground and thrust it into the back of shadow Lucius. The end of the staff penetrated his body and protruded from his chest. I could see Sylk tracing symbols in the air. Shadow Lucius stepped back and tried to remove the staff. The moment his hands touched it, I felt a thump hit my chest. The wind stopped blowing and there was a silent pause. For a brief moment everything stood still. Then a rumbling started deep in the ground and Sylk pulled me down as he traced the last symbol, enclosing us in a cylinder of silver light. It wasn't enough.

"Brace your—" he began.

The blast cut the cylinder of light, shredding it and throwing us back out of the circle and past what used to be the tree line of the garden. I could see Roman kneeling behind his hammer as the blast washed over him. Somehow he remained in place, but the blast scorched his skin raw. The chi of the plane was rebalancing. A convex shield of silver light had formed before us and I could see Sylk with his arm extended keeping it in place. The blast died down and I was about to stand up when he pulled me behind the wall of light.

"It's not over yet. Stay behind the wall," he said through gritted teeth.

Sweat was running down his face as he maintained the wall. Another thump punched me in the abdomen and sat me down. A stronger wave of energy and fire rushed past us. His robes fluttered behind him. It felt like sitting in a wind tunnel with hurricane force winds swirling around you. I threw myself on my stomach and stayed there. When the second blast stopped I could see that Sylk held his right arm to his chest.

"It's broken," he said matter of factly.

We had just managed to survive the equivalent of a small-scale nuclear explosion and he had a broken arm. *Note to self:do not piss Sylk off.* I looked around us and noticed the earth was scorched. In some places I noticed patches of glass.

We headed back to the circle and I realized we were much farther than I thought. It took us a good two minutes before we reached the edge of the circle where Roman stood. His hammer was on the ground next to him and he looked into the center of the circle where a figure lay.

"The shadow lingers," said Roman.

I couldn't believe my eyes. Shadow Lucius had not been destroyed by the blast. When we got closer I could see he had a gaping hole in his chest and he wasn't moving.

"Is he dead?" I said.

"He was never alive," said Roman. He moved the figure with his boot and the shadow's eyes fluttered.

"You cannot hide the ascendants indefinitely. They will need to return to the hub or the barriers will fall. When they do, my Harbinger will destroy them," said the shadow.

"We will stop Rael and send him back to join you," said Sylk.

"He cannot die. I have ensured it. You will fail and then I will be free. I will find you. Your pain will be of the highest order, my child, and I will bathe in your agony," said the shadow.

"We will create more ascendants, more than your Harbinger can kill. We have a core ascendant now. You have failed, destroyer," said Roman.

The shadow began to laugh. "He is useless to you. I seared his ability to access his chi. He is a fallen warrior now, good for nothing except a quick death."

The shadow began turning transparent.

"What you have done can be undone," said Roman.

"Not by anyone alive today — not even the Samadhi can undo my work. Not even you of my bloodline," he said, looking at Sylk.

"We shall see, destroyer," said Roman.

The shadow was almost gone now. I could see the ground clearly under its body.

"The next time we meet, warrior, I will be merciful and make your death swift," said the shadow as it disappeared.

"We must leave this place. He will regain his strength in time. I do not look forward to facing him again," said Roman.

"How do you propose we do that? The tré is gone. Even if it weren't I can't make a portal until my arm is healed," said Sylk.

I looked back and only a vague outline remained of what was the golden tré. The two inner concentric circles had vanished and the third outer circle was in broken sections.

"I don't have the energy to get us back. That blast took all I had left," said Roman.

"Can we use this?" I said as I fished out the area wide retriever.

Sylk held out his hand and I placed it in his palm.

"How did you get this?" he said.

"Devin gave it to me in the dojo, right before Rael brought me here."

"Devin? I thought him dead," said Sylk as he looked at Roman.

"I gave him a good pounding, but I didn't kill him. He left the hall of Sherfym before I could hit him further. I always did enjoy our fights," said Roman as he swung his hammer over his shoulder. "Will this work? Devin was always a clever one."

"Who is it keyed to? I don't want to end up in the middle of another fight for my life. One group of ever-spawning Gyrevex is an experience I would not like to revisit," said Sylk as he handed the retriever back to me.

"It's keyed to Meja. Where is she?" I said.

Sylk moved me to the center of what used to be the tré.

"Use it here. The latent energy should give it the boost we need. I hope," said Sylk.

"You hope?" I said.

Behind Sylk, Roman nodded.

"This is the lost triad. The connection to these planes has been severed. The energy needed…" said Roman.

"We need a lot of energy to get in and even more to get out of this place. I don't know if that has enough in it for all of us. I still don't know how the Keeper did it," said Sylk.

I had to 'kill' Rael before the portal worked before.

Two of the blue clad figures joined us in the circle. I saw that one of them was Adra. She nodded at me.

"Felix?" said Roman.

Adra shook her head. "The Gyrevex, sir."

Roman nodded, his face grim.

"Hand it to me, warrior," said Sylk. "Gather close and maintain contact."

We stood close to each other making sure we touched one another. Sylk placed the card in his broken right hand pressed his thumb down on the depression. He sent his chi down his arm and the lines flared silver as the rectangle flashed blue once and transported us.

FORTY-SIX

THE HEALER WAS ADJUSTING vials when the group appeared. She gave a curt nod to Sylk. "Alpha. Who be these?"

She eyed the hammer that Roman carried and stepped close to him.

"This is the warrior, Dante, and this is—"

"You be the hammer?" she interrupted. "Many of my people have fallen before that weapon."

"Only in battle, and many times it was chance that spared me from the dreaded Rah Ven time skipping," said Roman.

She snorted. "You have been lucky. Death in battle is honorable. I'll hold no grudge if my people died as warriors should. There are others with kin in the Watch who are not as forgiving. Do not tarry here. Not even the alpha can prevent a drawing of claws for the fallen," she said, looking at Sylk.

"I'll not abuse your hospitality and I do not wish to bring you any trouble. I can reach my plane from here. The warrior and I will take our leave," said Roman.

"Give me a moment," I said as I walked over to Meja's bed.

I looked over at the others and saw Luna, Samir, Zen and Kal all getting the same treatment. *Kal wasn't with us when the Lotus attacked.*

"When did Kal get injured? The Lotus didn't hit her with poison," I said.

The healer threw her hands up in exasperation.

"Grandmother…" said Sylk.

"She forced my hand, alpha. Said she wasn't leaving without his body." She pointed at Zen. "I had to tell truth. Not used to twisting stories. My words are straight, like blood follows the cut," she said as she fussed with her bottles.

"What did you do?" said Sylk.

"She chose. I explained it all, down to the last drop. She chose to become like him to stay with him," she said.

"Like him? What happened to Zen?" I said.

"The Lotus poison was too much for his system. It was either let him die or turn him," said Sylk.

"Into what?"

"He is part Rah Ven now. So is she. They don't belong to your world anymore," said the healer in my face. "They will have to stay here until the change is complete."

Zen and Kal, part Rah Ven?

She stood still and began to sniff the air.

"Cane's dogs, alpha. If they find the hammer here they will attack."

"Understood. Let's go, warrior," said Roman.

I turned to Sylk. "Thank you. If you hadn't—"

"I was saving my life. You just happened to be close by, warrior. No thanks are needed," he said.

"Will you tell her that Devin is alive? I'm sure she will want to know that," I said.

"I will," said Sylk.

"We will meet again in a few days. I will organize a group to pursue Rael. He won't be able to hide for long, not from me. Where can I find you?" said Roman.

"I have some questions to ask the Mikai. I will meet you in Aurora's passage in five days," said Sylk.

"Agreed. In five days, then."

Roman touched his hammer to the floor several times and a portal opened in front of us. Adra and her companion stepped through, disappearing from view. I turned to walk through and felt the rectangle in my outer pants pocket.

"Here, you may need this more than I will," I said as I handed Mariko's fan to Sylk.

He took it and nodded to me.

Roman stepped through, I took one look back and I followed him into uncertainty.

FORTY-SEVEN

SYLK OPENED A PORTAL INTO the nexus dojo. He placed Meja and Samir in beds and waited. Mara stood behind him and to the right, daggers in her hands. Her body was a coiled spring ready to attack.

"Relax, Mara. I don't expect Devin will launch an attack as we deliver his sister and the syllabist to him. His wife, on the other hand…"

"Yes, Master," she said.

Moments passed and the door opened. Mara tensed until she saw it was Devin. She let out a breath and held it when she saw Monique. She took a step closer to Sylk, ready to strike. The tension between the women was palpable. Monique had her daggers in hand as well, their edges glistening with poison.

Sylk raised his hand signaling to Mara. She lowered her weapons but didn't sheath them. Sylk removed a book from the inner pocket of his robe and handed it to Devin.

Devin nodded as he accepted the book. "The master syllabist text?" he said.

"As agreed. A dangerous text in the best of times. Do you think you can keep it safe? We will need it soon," said Sylk.

"How are they?" said Devin ignoring the gibe as he looked at Meja and Samir in their beds.

"They will recover. Zen and Kal will stay with Luna, a Rah Ven, until their period of adjustment is over."

"She really chose to turn?"

"He didn't have a choice, but she did. I hope being by his side will ease the transition into his new life. Dante will need a new guardian," said Sylk.

"And Dante is?"

"With Aurora. Lucius, or rather his shadow, seared his access to his chi."

"He's fallen? Can she help him? I have never heard of anyone recovering from something like that in the past," said Devin.

"If anyone can help him, she can. She is skilled in her ability, perhaps only second to Lucius himself. He didn't receive expert instruction here."

Devin bristled but remained calm. Monique came up on the balls of her feet. Mara did the same as the temperature of the room dropped a few degrees.

"He wasn't here long enough to learn much before your disciple kidnapped him," said Devin with a smile that never reached his eyes. "How *is* Anna these days?"

"Dead. Watchers erased her," said Sylk with a hard edge.

"I wish I could say I was sorry. You forced him into a manifestation before he was ready."

"I tried to help him manifest his weapon so we could meet the threat of Lucius prepared, unlike the Order of Warriors."

"And yet he manages to manifest one of the deadliest weapons in existence. How did that happen, *Karashihan*?"

"That wasn't supposed to happen. I don't know. I don't know if he picked the weapon or it him," said Sylk.

"What about the weapon? Where is it?"

"With Lucius."

"How, I thought Dante was fallen?"

"Lucius, or rather his shadow, stripped it from the warrior."

"I see," said Devin.

"There is still much to be done. The Harbinger is still loose. Aurora secured the ascendants, but not before the Gyrevex brought their number close to causing a barrier failure. She cannot hide them off-plane for too long before the connection is severed, causing the barrier to fall."

"They will have to come back to the hub eventually. We are trying to locate other core ascendants, but I'm afraid Dante may be the last one on this plane," said Devin.

"Much depends on the warrior, it would seem."

"Everything," said Devin. "Try not to get him killed."

"The last time I checked it was the Lotus that was doing the poisoning," said Sylk.

Monique took a step forward but Devin touched her arm, stopping her.

Sylk began to trace symbols in the air, his hand glowing silver as a portal opened behind him.

"I have some business with the Mikai. In a few days I will meet with Roman to discuss the Harbinger."

"Mikai, nasty business, that. I'm going to skip the meet with Roman if you don't mind. We didn't exactly end on a good note the last time we spoke."

"I wasn't inviting you, warrior. I would like this meeting to be productive. We have greater enemies to confront," said Sylk.

Sylk bowed to both of them. Mara stood beside him as they stepped back.

"Find him a guardian or train the one he has to do her job effectively," said Sylk, looking at Meja.

Devin remained silent as Sylk disappeared in to the portal.

Monique turned to Devin. "You should have let me cut him!" she said as she threw her dagger, burying it in the stone wall where the portal had been moments earlier.

"Ruining daggers is not the answer. Get that before someone else tries and ends up dead. We will deal with him later. Sylk and I have much to settle. Right now we have a Harbinger to hunt down," said Devin.

FORTY-EIGHT

WE EXITED THE PORTAL INTO a training area. Around us men and women engaged in different methods of combat. Some using weapons, others unarmed.

"Send word to Aurora we have arrived," said Roman to Adra. "Let me show you to your quarters, warrior. While here you will obey the rules of conduct. You will train as every other warrior does and you will have special training."

"Special training? What kind of special training?" I said.

He stopped walking and turned to face me.

"Let me explain something, in case you're confused about your purpose here. You can't access your chi. If you can't create other ascendants or manifest a weapon, what good are you?"

"I didn't need to access my chi against Lucius," I said.

He shook his head in disbelief.

"Do you think that was you? The only reason you were able to do what you did in the lost triad was because of the energy of the plane. That was not *your* chi. We got lucky. I don't depend on chance to carry me, despite what you may have heard," he said.

Adra came back and found us.

"She is ready for you, sir."

"Thank you. Go to debrief and I will meet you there in ten," said Roman.

We continued walking down several wide corridors. The space reminded me of the nexus dojo, only these corridors were well lit. We stood before two large metal blast doors. Each door could have secured a bank vault. The doors whispered open, revealing a thickness of three to four feet.

We walked past the doors into an expansive room. In front of an immense picture window sat a large mahogany desk covered in papers and documents. The other three walls were covered floor to ceiling in bookshelves. There was a plush burgundy and gold flecked carpet covering the floor. An intricate design filled the center of it but was covered by the desk. The room smelled of old paper with a hint of wood and citrus.

Beside the desk stood a tall woman in blue monitor robes holding a clipboard and jotting down notes. Her face was obscured by her hood. She didn't look up as we entered.

Behind the desk sat a woman who exuded strength. I could tell she was used to a position of authority by her posture. She sat ramrod straight in her chair with an air of quiet confidence. Around her, assistants came and went while she handed papers to one and took sheets from another, making notations and handing the sheet back. I couldn't sense her level of chi or any chi for that matter, but I could tell she had power. It radiated from her.

She looked up from her papers, removed her glasses and scrutinized me.

"Is this he?" she said.

"Yes ma'am, it took some doing but here he is. He has been seared. Lucius has made him one of the fallen," said Roman.

She sighed in response and pinched the bridge of her nose.

"A fallen warrior. Goddamn you, Lucius," she said under her breath while she stood, placing both hands on the desk. She wasn't a tall woman. Her muscular frame gave me the impression of size. Her black hair, pulled back in a bun, gave her a severe look. She wore a simple sleeveless blue robe patterned after the monitors of the nexus dojo. It reminded me of a hadajuban—the clothing worn under a kimono. We stood before her desk as she looked at me. What stopped the air in my lungs were her eyes. They were gray, like storm clouds pregnant with rain. Exactly like Lucius.

"My inner sight tells me you have potential. It also tells me that to undo this will take time— time we do not have. Are you certain he is a core ascendant?" she said to Roman.

"Yes, ma'am, he manifested one of the three foci with little to no training," said Roman.

"Impressive, but that alone will not be enough. You met the shadow, yes?"

I swallowed. My mouth had become a desert. "Yes, ma'am," I said.

"What you encountered was not one tenth of his power. I don't think anyone has or ever will reach that level of power again. Did you explain the training?" she said to Roman.

"No, ma'am. I felt that would be better left to you," he said.

She looked at me then, as if gauging how much she could say. Her eyes looked right through me.

"Very well. We need ascendants. Specifically, I need you to create more ascendants. I don't have the time it takes to undo the searing the way it should be done. That would take months, years. That is time we don't have. Done my way, it will be painful. It will be agony. When you think the pain is about to subside it will be even more pain, more than you have ever withstood in your life. If you thought the searing was difficult, the undoing will make that feel comfortable in comparison."

"Yes, ma'am," I managed. I remembered being suspended in that light and the unbearable pain.

"Now you have a choice, ascendant. You can have me reverse the damage done to you while experiencing soul-crushing pain. You will wish you were dead many times over while you undergo this process. Or, I can kill you now and save us both the trouble. What will it be?"

Roman had stepped away from me as she spoke her last words. I turned to see him standing across the room, looking at me. When I looked back at Aurora her eyes were glowing with a deep golden light. For a moment I stood there dumbfounded, until Roman coughed and brought me back.

"I will undergo the process, ma'am," I croaked. My voice had betrayed me.

"Speak up, ascendant," she said.

"I will undergo the process, ma'am," I said with force.

She looked at Roman and handed her assistant a sheet of paper. The glow had left her eyes.

"Get him prepped within the hour. We have no time to lose." She turned to face me. "Welcome to your unmaking, ascendant. I hope you survive it," she said and turned back to her assistants.

FORTY-NINE

RAEL STOOD OUTSIDE THE dojo. It had been difficult to find ascendants the last few days. Most of the dojos were stranded. He had unleashed the Gyrevex to hunt and kill as many as they could find. He could sense an ascendant in this one.

"Maybe this one will be a challenge. What do you think?" he said to the Gyrevex beside him. The Gyrevex remained silent. "Why do I even bother?"

One Gyrevex remained behind as he climbed to the second level. The second followed him with silent menace. When he reached the top of the stairs he unsheathed his swords. He pushed open the door and stood in the middle of an empty dojo floor. In the corner a figure slept. Dressed in rags and old clothing, the old man snored while Rael crossed the dojo floor, oblivious to the noise.

"Hello? Anyone home? I'm here to kill you," he said as his voice echoed off the walls. "Hmm, maybe they left recently. I could be sensing residual chi."

He looked around, finding nothing else of importance and turned to leave as the doors slammed shut.

"Oh look, a trap. Now I'm really in danger. What will I do now? Really, this never gets old," he said as he turned to face the 'homeless' man, who had been sleeping in the corner, sheathing his swords.

"Hello, Harbinger — or should I call you Rael?" said the old man.

Rael squinted in the dim light trying to make out the features of the man in front of him.

"That voice. I know you. Sensei Wei. Sensei Wu Wei. You aren't an ascendant. I barely sense any chi from you at all. What are you doing here? Have you grown tired of life?"

"I'm here to stop you. Your master will not be free."

"You can't kill me. Those more powerful than you have tried, and failed. The only way you are going to stop me is to kill me, which can't be done. Do I need to go on?"

"I can see you have not changed with age— still impudent, arrogant and short sighted," said Wei. "Let me open your eyes."

He cast off the rags and old coat and was dressed in a simple silk uniform.

"Not seeing much, except a quick change. Well done, by the way," said Rael.

Rael gestured at the Gyrevex.

"He wants to fight, give him one. Make it fast, we have ascendants to kill."

The Gyrevex closed in, spinning the bell. It took two quick steps and launched the bell at the sensei. Wei bent backwards and allowed the bell to ride his arms as he redirected it back to the Gyrevex. It was the last thing it expected as the bell slammed into it, causing it to stumble back and impact a wall. Wei ran up to the off balanced Gyrevex and placed a hand on its chest. The Gyrevex tried to step away as Wei absorbed its essence, causing it to vanish.

"A prime ascendant. I thought you were all wiped out with the purge of the Iman line?" said Rael as he drew his swords. Their energy filled the dojo around him.

"I still remain," said Wei, taking a defensive stance.

Rael advanced, letting the energy flow free from his swords. Wei stood still and let him come. Rael lifted both swords and slashed on a diagonal. Wei ducked the slash and stepped around Rael, touching him a number of times. Each time he touched Rael, less energy escaped the swords. Rael thrusted forward with one sword while holding the other back. Wei slapped the flat of the blade, shattering it. He followed the hilt down to Rael's arm and struck his wrist, causing him to drop what remained of his sword. Rael attacked with the other sword and Wei slid to the side and trapped Rael's arm, forcing him to miss and toss the remaining sword.

Wei began to drain Rael of chi. Rael collapsed to the floor as Wei held his arms.

"Are you strong enough to kill me, sensei?"

"I'm not going to kill you...now," said Wei.

Three members of the Black Lotus came from the side and placed suppression bands around Rael's forearms.

"I will inform Roman of our success," said Wei.

"No need," said Monique as she entered the dojo. "We have just the place for him. Take him to the box," she said to the members of her group.

A portal opened beside Rael as he was transported away.

"That was not the agreement," said Wei.

"The Warriors of the Way will hold this threat. We are not at cross purposes. Our goal is the same," she said.

"I advise against this, monitor," said Wei as he put on his old clothes and headed out for the door. "He would be better contained among Roman and his mistress."

"Those rogues are not equipped to deal with a threat of this magnitude. We will handle it and I will explain it to Roman," she said.

"I must go. I cannot linger in any one place for too long. Consider my words. I urge you to reconsider," said Wei as he left. She stood facing him, her expression hard.

"The decision has been made," she said.

Wei vanished into the night.

FIFTY

RAEL SAT IN THE BOX COUNTING bricks as dark smoke wafted in. The smoke travelled to the center and solidified. A shadow of Lucius stood in the box with Rael.

"Did you locate him?" said the shadow.

"Yes, a prime ascendant lives. Just as you predicted," said Rael.

"With him I can locate the second foci and be one step closer to our goal."

"Your goal, Master," said Rael.

"Yes, my goal. Once my work is complete I will grant you release. Until then you must play this ruse a little while longer. I have a question for you. Not too long ago you saved a girl. Young, maybe three or four."

Rael's chest tightened and he remained still. "Yes, a child was in the dojo when I dispatched the Fan." *Little Nina. I gave you my word, sensei. A life for a life.*

"What became of her?" said the shadow looking at Rael intently.

"I took care of her," said Rael.

He let the words remain between them. The shadow looked at Rael for a long moment as their eyes locked.

"Nothing and no one will be allowed to deter my purpose. Do you understand?"

"I understand," said Rael.

With a shift and a twist he took off the suppressor bands and put them to the side and rubbed his forearms.

"This chafes, Master."

"Once I have the three foci, I will erase the Warriors of the Way and bring a benevolent rule to the planes. They will see that my way is the better way. They will accept it or die," said the shadow as it drifted into nothingness, leaving Rael alone.

"I'll choose death," said Rael.

END OF BOOK TWO

Thank you for joining me, please share with family and friends. It would be great if you could leave me a review wherever you purchased the story. Thank you, your reviews help!

Please visit my blog, leave a comment and join my email list.

I look forward to hearing from you.

Other titles by Orlando Sanchez

The Spiritual Warriors

Blur-A John Kane Novel

The Deepest Cut-A Blur Short

The Last Dance A Sepia Blue Short

Connect with me online:

Blog: http://nascentnovel.com/

Facebook:
https://www.facebook.com/OSanchezAuthor

Twitter: https://twitter.com/SenseiOrlando

About the Author:

Orlando Sanchez has been writing ever since his teens when he was immersed in playing Dungeon and Dragons with his friends every weekend. An avid reader, his influences are too numerous to list here.

Aside from writing, his passion is the martial arts; he currently holds a 2nd Dan and 3rd Dan in two styles of Karate. If not training, he is studying some aspect of the martial arts or martial arts philosophy, or writing in his blog. For more information on the dojo he trains at, please visit www.mkdkarate.com

Made in the USA
Columbia, SC
09 November 2024

46066682R00138